THE LAST MISSION

War is Hell ... but Peacetime'll kill you!

General Patton completely endorsed that old soldiers' saying. The carnage of World War II was over: peace had just been declared, but Patton determined to continue his war against the Russians. The threat of Communism loomed over Eastern Europe as the wily General Ulanov plotted the first blow in his megalomaniac invasion campaign – to massacre the remainder of the Hungarian Army. Patton had to act fast and he sent in T-Force ... with orders to ignore the cease-fire and stop at nothing! The war might well be over, but there was plenty more violent action ahead for the General's private army.

T-FORCE:
THE LAST MISSION

T-Force: The Last Mission

by

Charles Whiting

Dales Large Print Books
Long Preston, North Yorkshire,
BD23 4ND, England.

British Library Cataloguing in Publication Data.

Whiting, Charles
T-force: the last mission.

A catalogue record of this book is
available from the British Library

ISBN 978-1-84262-571-2 pbk

First published in Great Britain in 1979
by Severn House Publishers

Published in Large Print 2007 by arrangement with
Eskdale Publishing

Dales Large Print is an imprint of Library Magna Books Ltd.

Printed and bound in Great Britain by
T.J. (International) Ltd., Cornwall, PL28 8RW

'War is hell, but peacetime'll kill you!'
Old Soldiers' Saying.

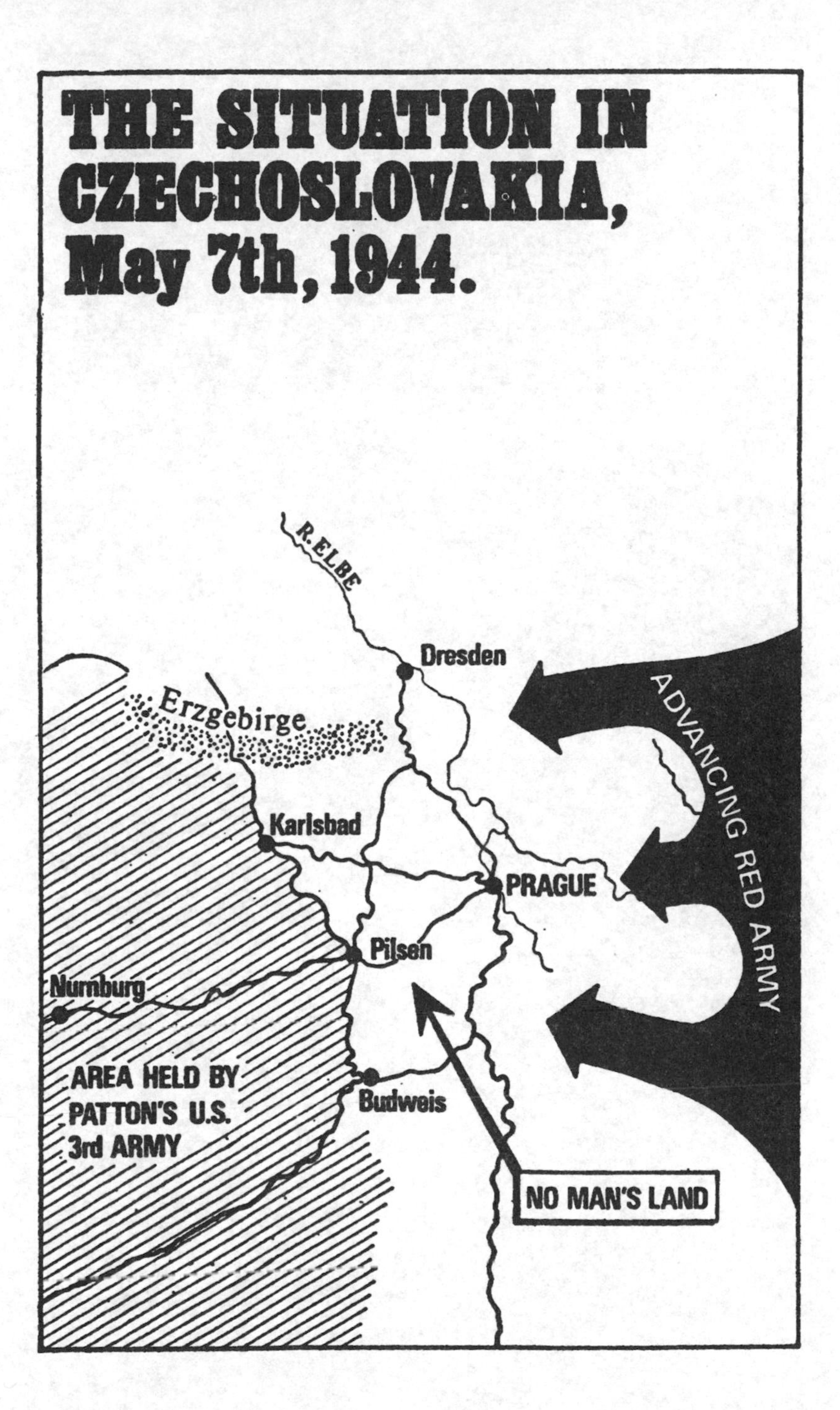
THE SITUATION IN CZECHOSLOVAKIA, May 7th, 1944.
R.ELBE
Dresden
Erzgebirge
Karlsbad
PRAGUE
Pilsen
Nurnburg
Budweis
AREA HELD BY PATTON'S U.S. 3rd ARMY
ADVANCING RED ARMY
NO MAN'S LAND

DAY ONE

'Give me a couple of days in Prague and I'll have enough incidents with those sons-of-bitches that the folks back home will be screaming out for a shooting war with the Red bastards!'

Gen. George Patton to Gen. Bradley
May 6th, 1945.

ONE

The dust-covered American half-track rattled to a stop. With a sigh of relief, a red-faced Wheels turned off the ignition. Behind him vehicle after vehicle of the US Third Army's T-Force came to a halt on the glaring white road to the Czech border, opposite the group of command vehicles drawn up under the protection of the flak half-tracks in a circle around them. Gratefully the men of the Third Army's élite long-range reconnaissance force slumped back in the metal seats. It had been a long morning.

Wearily Major Hardt, T-Force's CO, dropped over the side of the half-track and made his way stiffly towards the brass. They were grouped around the tall, elegant figure of the Army Commander in his lacquered helmet, its three outsize golden stars gleaming in the spring sunshine.

General George Patton saw him coming. He dropped his 'warface' and beamed. Obviously, Hardt thought, the Old Man was in high good humour at the prospect of the new campaign in Czechoslovakia.

'Well,' he bellowed in his thin high voice, over the sudden roar of a squadron of Mustangs zooming high into the bright blue sky, 'how does it look up there, son?'

Major Hardt saluted and then wiped the back of his hand across his dust-stained face. 'It's crazy, sir. Crazy as hell! The whole Kraut front has broken. SS divisions, Cossacks, Rumanians, Hungarians – they're all bugging out before the Russians can grab them! A real snafu. The Czech patriots are sniping them and they're sniping each other. We got fired on twice. Nothing serious.' With a nod of his head he indicated the bandaged soldier sitting up in the cab of the second half-track. 'They just winged him.'

'Regular Kraut troops?' Patton asked.

'No, sir. The Kraut army has had it. Even the SS is not fighting back. My guess is that it was either a bunch of Czech patriots who didn't realise that we were Americans, or some of those goddam Kraut Werewolves we've been hearing about of late.'

'A rabble of dumb Kraut kids in short pants,' Patton snorted contemptuously. 'They want their skinny Kraut asses paddling and sending back to their mothers. No matter.' He jerked his thin face forward eagerly.

'What of Prague, son?'

'The main highway right up to the capital is wide open, sir. The patriots have taken over the suburbs everywhere. They're just waiting for us to make a triumphal entry. Prague is the Third Army's for the taking!'

Exuberantly Patton slapped his riding crop against his gleaming, handmade riding boots and swung round to his staff. 'Did you hear that, gentlemen?' he cried excitedly. 'Prague is ours for the taking! It's just what I predicted.'

Another squadron of Mustangs, heading for the new front, roared over their heads at tree-top height; but General Patton was too excited by Major Hardt's news to notice. 'Kay, we didn't get Berlin and we didn't get Vienna,' he continued at the top of his voice, 'and I don't need to tell you why not. Those jerks at Supreme Headquarters haven't gotten the message that you can't pussy-foot with the Russkis. But we're not gonna hand 'em Prague on a silver plate like we did the other two capitals. No sir! God willing and with a little bit of luck the Third Army will be in Prague by this time tomorrow afternoon!' He grinned suddenly, showing his dingy, sawn-off teeth. 'Hell, how are you gonna stop those Joes of mine? The Czechs are our allies and their women aren't off-limits like the Kraut women back there in Germany. *On to Prague and fraternization!* How can you stop an army which has a battle cry like that?'

His staff officers grinned. They knew the Old Man. Patton wouldn't be beyond publishing the battle cry as an official order-of-the-day. And it would work too. The Third Army's sex-starved GIs would go barrelling all the way to Prague, regardless of the opposition and danger, lured on by the prospect of getting into the hay with some plump Prague pigeon.

Patton's grin vanished as abruptly as it had come. 'Codman,' he bellowed at his smiling senior aide. 'Take that goddam obscene grin off your face and get me General Bradley on the phone. At the double!'

Swiftly Patton sketched in his dispositions to his boss, General Bradley, in far-off Frankfurt, concluding with the words: 'Brad, my lead troops are eighty miles from Prague. The main highway is wide open. I've alerted the Fourth Armoured Division and those boys are eager to go. Shit, they'd go through what is left of the Kraut resistance in front of us like a dose of senna pods through a fat whore!'

But the cautious ex-infantryman, who now commanded all the American land forces in Europe, was not so excited by the prospect of capturing the Czech capital as his subordinate. 'Listen, Georgie,' he explained in his slow Missouri accent, 'you know the Supreme Commander's instructions? They're explicit enough. The stop line for the US Army in Czechoslovakia is Pilsen, sixty miles from Prague. Ike doesn't want our troops to start tangling with the Red Army advancing from the east.'

Patton muttered an obscenity. 'Brad,' he pleaded, 'just let me get lost for one single day. I'll stay incommunicado for a day. Tell Ike you can't find me. Then I'll report that I've captured Prague.' He chuckled suddenly. 'From a telephone booth in the capital's main square! What will Ike be able to do then – give the goddam place back to the Krauts?'

Bradley remained firm. 'The halt-line through Pilsen is mandatory for V and XII Corps, Georgie. Moreover you must not – I repeat, *not* – reconnoitre to a greater depth than five miles north-east of Pilsen. Ike doesn't want any international complications at this late date. Hell, you must understand that, Georgie, we've just about finished one war with the Krauts. We don't want to start another one with the Russians over some crackpot little country like Czechoslovakia.'

'For God's sake, Brad,' Patton cried angrily. 'It seems to me that a great nation like America should let others worry about the complications. Hell,' he exploded, 'what do we care what those goddam Russians think! We're gonna have to fight them sooner or later, within the next generation. Why not do it now while our Army is intact and the damn Russkis can have their hind ends kicked back into Russia in three months. We can do it ourselves and if we need help we can set the Krauts on 'em. They hate the bastards just as I do!'

Patton paused for breath, his thin face flushed a hectic red. At the other end, General Bradley gasped with shock. 'Shut up, Georgie, you fool!' he ordered. 'For all we goddam know, the Russians might be picking this up on short wave. Talk like that can start another war, don't you know that?'

Patton refused to shut up. Outside, he could see the clouds of thick white dust as the first Shermans of the Fourth Armoured started to roll towards Pilsen, their decks heavy with confident grinning armoured infantrymen. Instinctively he knew those same men could be entering Prague as conquerors within the next twenty-four hours, if they got the green light from above. 'Hell, Brad. Let's start a war with the Russians *now.* Give me a couple of days in Prague and I'll have enough incidents with those sons-of-bitches that the folks back home will be screaming out for a shooting war with the Red bastards. You don't have to get mixed up with it at all if you're so damn soft about it and scared of your rank. Just let me handle it down here. I'll get you your war.'

'George,' Bradley cried at the other end in utter disbelief, 'you must be crazy! *Attack the Russians?* Where in Sam Hill do you get such goddam ideas?' He hurried on before Patton could protest. 'Now understand this – Pilsen is the stop line for the Third Army, with recon to a depth of five miles to the north-east.' He calmed himself with difficulty. 'George get this, once you reach Pilsen, the shooting war is over for you. Kay?'

'But–'

'There are no buts!' Bradley snapped firmly. 'Pilsen is it for General George S. Patton.' And with that, the Army Group Commander rammed down the radio phone. Suddenly the line went dead in Patton's hand.

Slowly, very slowly, the tall, white-haired General turned to his expectant, waiting staff. He shook his head. 'No deal, gentlemen,' he announced in a low voice. 'General Bradley won't authorize a drive to Prague.' He sighed. 'We gonna have to leave it to the Russians for the taking!'

He placed his gleaming helmet on his white head. With his broad shoulders slumped like those of a beaten old man, he started to walk to the waiting jeep, which would drive him to Pilsen. In silence, his suddenly subdued staff followed him, shuffling their gleaming riding boots through the thick white dust.

For a moment Major Hardt watched them, telling himself that it looked as if Old Blood an' Guts Patton's fighting days were about over. Then he pulled himself together. T-Force would be needed to lead the drive to the Czech city, just in case the Werewolves tried to take a pot shot at the Commanding General as they rode through the foothills.

'Kay, Wheels,' he snapped at the little ex-New York cabbie who had been his driver since he had first organised T-Force back in North Africa in 1942. 'Roll 'em!'

'And what's our objective, skipper?' Van

Fleet, his handsome socialite Exec, asked.

'Pilsen,' Hardt barked above the roar of the engines starting all along the length of the column.

'And then?'

'Then – *nowhere!* That's the stop-line. For the Third Army, the war stops once we get there.'

'Kiss me quick, me muvver's drunk.' Limey, T-Force's Cockney radio operator, yelled exuberantly as the half-track began to edge its way forward onto the road which led to Pilsen. '*Peacetime!*'

TWO

The Third Army's armour, led by T-Force, entered the Czech beer town of Pilsen that night. But General Patton, his face pale and taut, did not see the wildly happy faces of the cheering throngs of flower-throwing Czechs, free after six years of Nazi rule, nor hear the thunderous chant of '*Patton! … Patton! … Patton!*'

For him this was the last day of the battle. He was nearly sixty years of age, old as fighting generals went. In spite of his brilliant combat record in the last eleven months, he knew he had stepped on too many toes. A lot of important people both in Europe and Washington didn't like him; they would use his age to prevent him from getting another active command in the Pacific.

'Goddamnit, Hardt,' he said to the T-Force Commander as he entered the Pilsen hotel, which would be Patton's HQ for the next few days, 'it looks as if I'm gonna die with my boots off and in bed after all, and not on the battlefield.' He shook his head wearily. 'Just like some lousy two-bit pimp in a cathouse who's whored himself to death.'

Hardt refrained from smiling at Patton's colourful choice of phrase. He knew what the Old Man must be feeling at this moment. The shooting had stopped too abruptly for him. Perhaps it had for all of them after the dangerous, yet heady excitement of four years of war. But for Patton the let-down was tremendous. It showed in the features of his lined face.

'Son,' Patton began, 'I love war. Peacetime is gonna be hell for me–'

'General.' It was Codman, his chief aide.

'What is it, Charley?'

By way of an answer, Colonel Codman

gestured to the little group of men entering the lobby in a strange uniform which Hardt couldn't identify for a moment. Then he recognised the dark dress uniform and massive epaulettes of the Red Army.

'Who are these men?' Patton asked, shaken out of his sad reverie by the sudden appearance of Russians in the newly occupied Czech town.

'The Red Army Liaison Team from the 1st Ukrainian Front advancing on Prague from the East. The big one with all the medals,' Codman lowered his correct Bostonian voice, 'is General Ulanov, the head of the team. He would like to take a drink with you and explain how he is going to work his mission so that there will be no clashes between their men and ours when the Red Army reaches Pilsen.'

Patton breathed out hard and took in the burly, shaven-headed Russian General, his tunic dripping with medals of all shapes and sizes, while Ulanov in turn regarded him warily with small, piglike eyes.

A long time seemed to pass, while Patton's staff officers stared at their Chief apprehensively, watching his 'number five frown' begin to cross his face: the frown he reserved for s.o.bs right at the bottom of his personal hate list.

'Tell him, Charley,' he broke silence at last, 'tell the Russian sonuvabitch that I'd rather cut my own throat at this moment than have a drink–' Patton's anger at being prevented from taking Prague, by Eisenhower's concern that a clash with the Russians must be avoided at all costs, welled up in full vehemence. 'Tell him to go and jump in the goddam river!'

Codman's face paled. 'I am sorry, sir, but I cannot tell the General that.'

But he didn't need to. Ulanov understood. The look on Patton's face had sufficed. He bowed stiffly at the waist and without a word turned angrily and stalked out, followed by his bewildered officers.

Hardt repressed a grin at the Russian General's discomfiture. While a harassed Codman hurried after the Russians, presumably to help them find quarters for the night, he turned to follow. But he never reached the door. Patton's high-pitched voice stopped him.

'Just where the Sam Hill do you think you're going, Major?'

'I thought I'd hit the sack, sir.'

'Why?' Patton demanded.

'It's been a very long day,' Hardt

answered. 'I'm pretty pooped, sir.'

'The hell you're pooped,' Patton snarled. 'I need company. You're not going to hit the sack just yet. Go up to my room. You'll find a bottle of bourbon in my footlocker. Take it and a handful of cigars and come to my office. We're gonna drink that whisky and smoke those cigars and then you can go to bed. Snap to, Major – that's an order!'

All tiredness gone, Hardt snapped to. He knew there was no refusing the Commanding General of the Third Army in his present black mood.

Outside now the sound of the cheering had died away to be replaced by the snap and crackle of small arms fire, as the Czech patriots let off their newly captured German weapons. The drunken bawling of GIs who had sampled too much of the good Pilsener beer and were now looking for women, unrestricted by the Eisenhower Non-Fraternization ban added to the noise.

Patton pointed a long cigar at the open window through which the wild confusion of Czech and American voices came and said: 'Let them get on with it this night. They deserve it. Anything my Joes of the Third Army have fought for they're entitled to have, by God!' He took another drink of the fiery bourbon. 'You know, son, I've always believed that – and I've never been proved wrong yet – that a man who won't fuck, won't fight.'

Hardt nodded, but remained silent. Under the influence of the alcohol, the General was simmering down, he could see that. All the same he had not yet thrown off the bitterness of this day – the last he would ever command a fighting army.

'You see, son,' Patton continued after a while. 'A man has got to have a powerful drive in this life to get anywhere. He has to be single-minded, especially if he is an officer, commanding other men, going for the one thing on which he has decided. Naturally if you're like that, you'll make some people miserable. But you can't make an omelette without cracking eggs, as the French say.'

Hardt nodded encouragingly. The Old Man was not conducting a dialogue with him, but a monologue. It was better not to interrupt.

'And when it looks, son,' Patton continued after another sip of bourbon, 'as if you're getting close to your objective, whatever it is, all kinds of people, even some you thought were loyal friends, will suddenly start doing their hypocritical God-damnedest to do you down, bad-mouth you, put obstacles in your way, break your spirit. Politicians are the goddam worst. Sure enough they'll wear Old Glory in public, but in order to win a few more votes in the caucus room, they'll wipe their ass on the flag of their own country. Look at the situation here now. There was nothing to stop us. The Krauts were beaten. We have fresh divisions itching to get into action. We have complete mastery of the air. We could march into any country in Central Europe and the local populace would welcome us with flowers. Even the Krauts these last few weeks have cheered my men when they've taken their cities. Why? Because they're goddam glad it's the Americans who are taking them over and not the Russians. But what do those dummies in Washington do – those lousy politicos?'

Patton pointed his long cigar almost accusingly at the young Major with the terribly scarred, completely bald head (the result of a run-in with a German flame-thrower back in North Africa). 'I'll tell you. They stop us. In case we offend the lousy Russians! They don't realise that from Genghis Khan to Stalin, they've never changed. They want power and territory. And whenever they find weakness, they take over.' He laughed bitterly. 'Goddamnit, what innocents those guys back in Washington must be, not to realise that whatever the Reds get their dirty Mongolian paws on they never let go of! But I'll tell you one thing, son. If I don't get an active fighting command in the Pacific against the Japs, I'm gonna resign my commission and tell the people of my country–'

But Hardt never did learn what Patton was going to do in that particular eventuality. For just then there was a polite tap at the door to the office.

It was Codman. 'Sorry to interrupt you, General,' he said hastily. 'But I've got somebody here who might cheer you up with what he has to say.' He stood back and allowed an elderly, aristocratic looking officer in the uniform of the Hungarian Army to enter the room.

Patton stubbed out his cigar and rose to his feet. The Hungarian clicked his heels together in the Central European fashion and touched the fingers of his right hand to his gold-braided cap. 'Jerzy,' he announced in English, 'Colonel-General Jerzy, Commander Third Hungarian Army. Or what is left of it – sixteen thousand men to be exact.' He sighed a little wearily and Hardt could see the lines of strain beneath the Hungarian's dark eyes. 'General Patton, I wish you would do me the honour of accepting the surrender of my Army.'

Patton tugged at his jacket and stretched to his full height, abruptly very formal as he always was on such occasions. 'And where is your army located at the present moment, General?' he asked.

'With your permission?'

Patton nodded.

The Hungarian walked across the room to the big covered map which ran the length of one wall. He glanced enquiringly at Patton. Again the Third Army Commander nodded. There was no need to conceal the disposition of his Army now, even from the Hungarian, who was an ally of the Germans. The shooting war was over. The Hungarian General pulled the cord and revealed a large scale map of Czechoslovakia, covered with a mass of blue and red symbols indicating American and German troops. With an elegantly manicured fingernail, he tapped the map. 'Here, General,' he announced. 'That was the position of my HQ when I left it to motor to your headquarters this afternoon.'

'How far was it from Pilsen?' Patton

demanded eagerly, well aware that the announcement *Third Army Accepts Surrender of Hungarian Third Army* would hit the headlines back in the States.

'Some forty kilometres from Pilsen, on Highway 64,' the Hungarian answered, beaming too, already feeling perhaps that he had managed to save his Command from the advancing Russians in the nick of time.

Patton did a rapid calculation. Outside a group of drunken GIs were bawling out the song of the 'maiden who could never be satisfied'. Patton did not hear. His mind was on other things. 'But that's about twenty-five miles from here.' He shook his head slowly, regretfully. 'I'm afraid, General, that puts your Command out of my area.'

'What do you mean, sir?' the Hungarian asked, suddenly aware that something had gone wrong with his plans.

'I mean General,' Patton answered bitterly, 'that my superiors, in their infinite wisdom, have decided that the US Third Army will not venture more than five miles north-east of Pilsen. That is my stop line. So your Command is exactly twenty miles too far away. You will have to surrender to the Russians when they arrive, where you are presently located.'

But the Hungarian did not give up so easily. 'We fought the Communists in our country back in 1919. Now with the Germans we have fought them in Russia and all the way back here from Stalingrad to the Czech border. If you would accept my surrender now, I'm sure I could get my people into your lines before the Russians arrive. We have horse-drawn transport.'

Patton bit his bottom lip. 'You must understand my position, General. Where you are presently located is officially Red Army territory with effect this 6th May 1945. I'm afraid you already belong to the Russians.'

'But General Patton,' the Hungarian answered. 'I'm sure you – of all people – comprehend what they will do with us. It will mean death or enslavement for my officers.' He said the words without rancour or any other emotion, as if he were making a statement about the weather.

Patton said nothing.

'Besides other things, we have the Crown of St Stephen, the ancient symbol of Hungarian sovereignty, which must never fall into Communist hands, come what may.' He tried to smile but failed miserably. 'We also have with us the War Chest of the Third Army, some five million silver talers.

They would be a legitimate prize of war for your own Army. There are the doc–'

'General,' Patton interrupted him harshly. 'I cannot help you and that is that.' Not giving the Hungarian any further opportunity to protest, he turned to Codman and ordered. 'Ensure that the Colonel-General is fed and given a room for the night. See that he returns to his own Command promptly at zero eight hundred hours tomorrow morning.'

The Hungarian let his shoulders slump. He had lost. Touching his hand to his cap weakly, he said, 'Thank you, General, for your kindness in seeing me. And may I wish you luck for the future.'

'The same to you,' Patton said, letting his eyes fall to the ground, as if he were suddenly ashamed of himself.

'Goddamnit!' he cried after the Hungarian had gone and crashed his fist down on the table so that glasses rattled. 'Imagine having to send a fine soldier like that – a gentleman from top to toe – back to face certain death at the hands of slopeheads like that Ulanov sonuvabitch. Jesus Christ, it's enough to make you puke!' He looked bitterly at Hardt. 'What is it the Old Heads say? *War's hell, but peacetime'll kill you!'* Brother, aren't they just too right.' Savagely he seized his glass and drained it in one angry gulp. 'Kay, Hardt, that's it. The party's over. Get back to your command. I'll see you at breakfast.'

'Sir.' Hastily Hardt rose to his feet to carry out the order. But he was fated to see General Patton once again before that particular last night of the shooting war was over.

THREE

'Hardt, wake up!'

The voice seemed to come from far, far away. 'Hardt, damnit, open your eyes!'

Instinctively the T-Force Commander's hand slid into his bedroll where he always kept his forty-five. Then he recognised the voice as American and opened his eyes.

Codman, with his blouse open as if he had dressed hastily, was bending over him with a flashlight in his hand.

Roughly Hardt pushed the light away and growled. 'For God's sake, Colonel, what's up?' He licked his scummed lips. 'Jesus, it can't be more than two hours.'

'Zero three to be correct. But that doesn't worry the Old Man, you know that.'

'The Old Man!' Hardt woke up at once and completely. 'What's he doing up at this time of night?'

'I'll tell you,' Codman answered grimly. 'He's over at the hotel, shouting for you.'

'Why?' Hardt cried, unzipping his sleeping bag and feeling for his slacks.

'I don't know, Hardt. All I know is that the shit has hit the fan over there for some reason or other and he's madder than hell, hollering for you. So move it, Major.'

Hardt moved it.

Patton was waiting for the two of them in the second floor of the darkened hotel which housed the HQ. He was dressed in an ancient bathrobe, his white hair tousled, puffing angrily at a big cigar, in spite of the anxious looks of his personal physician Colonel Odom, who was standing next to him, little black bag in hand.

'What in hell's name were you guys doing?' he snapped. 'It took you so long I thought you were coming via Tokyo.'

'Now General,' Odom said warningly. 'It's not going to do your heart much good, getting excited like that and smoking those cigars. You know what–'

'I know, I know,' Patton interrupted. 'I shouldn't drink bourbon. I shouldn't smoke cigars. If you had your way, Charles, I shouldn't even fuck. But come, we've no time for that now. Hardt, follow me!'

Completely bewildered by the strange summons in the middle of the night, Codman and Hardt followed Patton and the Doctor along the dimly lit corridor to an oak door bearing the brass '00' sign, which Hardt knew signified a toilet and bath in Central Europe. But this must be a pretty goddam important latrine, he told himself, as he saw the two white-helmeted MPs standing outside it, rigidly at attention.

Patton nodded to Odom.

The Doctor took a key out of his pocket and carefully unlocked the door, while Patton snapped at the wooden-faced MPs, 'See that nobody comes in after us. Understand?'

'Sir!'

Patton passed through, followed by Odom. Then it was the two junior officers' turn. Odom waited till they were all inside. Closing the door carefully behind them, Odom snapped on the light.

Codman gave a gasp of horror, and Hardt

bit his lip to stop himself doing the same, just in time.

The big bath, resting on iron claw feet in the corner beyond the toilet, was filled almost up to the brim with a thick red liquid, which Hardt knew instinctively was human blood. One very pale, limp hand hung over the side.

'Show him, Charles,' Patton ordered, puffing hard at his cigar.

Colonel Odom rolled up his sleeves and put his hands into the thick red liquid gingerly. For a brief instant, he searched there for something. Then he found it. Grasping the head by the thick silver hair, he pulled the deathly pale face from the blood, which ran down the sunken cheeks like red tears. With his free hand he pressed in the false teeth which bulged from the gaping mouth.

'The Hungarian!' Hardt gasped.

'Yes, Colonel-General Jerzy,' Patton rasped. 'Condemned to death by General George Patton exactly five hours ago, if I recollect correctly!'

'Now, now, General, don't blame yourself,' Colonel Odom said soothingly and let the ghastly head sink back into the blood.

'But I do – *I do,*' Patton said bitterly. Hardt could see the tears begin to flood his faded blue eyes. 'I turned him down and the poor son-of-a-bitch saw no other way out. Fancy a fine soldier like that having to die like this in a cruddy stinking provincial hotel craphouse–' he broke off, as if he could say no more.

'What happened, sir?' Hardt asked.

Odom, who was attempting to dry his hands on the bathroom's already badly blood-stained towel, answered. 'Suicide. A typical Central European suicide.' He indicated a half empty bottle of liquor at the side of the bath. 'He ran himself a hot bath and sat soaking in it, drinking spirits. Then when he was sufficiently relaxed, he immersed his wrists in the water until the main arteries stood out on them.' He shrugged. 'A couple of swift slashes with his razor and the blood must have begun to pour out of them like out of a faucet.' He summed up with almost professional calm. 'It is a relatively painless way to die.'

'It's an ignoble way to die for a soldier! An ignoble way, do you hear!' Patton cried angrily. 'And I condemned him to it because I was scared of some goddam canteen commando back in Paris who has never heard a goddam shot fired in anger in his whole career! God, am I disgusted with myself at this moment!'

Odom nodded to Codman urgently. 'Okay, General, we're getting out of here. This thing is making you overwrought.'

'Overwrought!' Patton exploded, as Codman headed for the door. 'That isn't the word for it, Charles. I'm about to hit the damn roof. But I'll tell you this. I'm not going to stand for it. I'm going to see that that poor guy in the bath there is avenged. By God, am I! Hardt, as soon as we get out of here come straight to my office, I've got a mission for you. I'll show those lousy jerks that General George S. Patton has finished kissing ass. By God, I will!'

General Patton had recovered from his shock completely by the time he was ready to receive Hardt in his office. Still in his shabby woollen dressing gown, he had supervised the furtive removal of the dead General's body from the bathroom. Now the two MPs were busy digging a grave for the body in the dark garden by the side of the hotel. In an hour or so it would be light, but by that time the body would be interred and the site of the fresh grave covered with turf fetched from elsewhere. In the meantime Codman had been detailed to take the battered Mercedes in which the dead General had driven to beg so unsuccessfully for help, complete with driver, to the T-Force lines. Nobody, Patton had emphasised to the few staff officers in the know about the events of that night, must learn of the suicide. By the time the HQ and the still sleeping townsfolk began to stir, it must be thought that the Hungarian General had already departed to return to his own command.

'You see, son,' Patton explained now, 'I want everybody to think I turned him down flat, especially that goddam Russian slope-head Ulanov.' He leaned forward across the desk, his face hollowed out to a death's head in the light of the single lamp, and lowered his voice, as if the barrel-chested Russian might be outside the door listening to him. 'I've got a plan but it is essential that everybody thinks I have washed my hands of that poor Hungarian fellow.'

'A plan, sir?' Hardt echoed, noting that the Old Man's eyes were blazing with that old excitement that he had often seen in them before the start of a new battle or offensive.

'Yes, I was a sorry bastard to turn down that poor s.o.b. out there in the garden. I can't do anything about it now. But I *can* do something about his officers – and his men, too, of course.'

'You mean you're going to accept their surrender after all, sir?'

'No, not exactly.' Patton leaned back in his chair, his face in the shadows again. 'You remember that Kraut General – Model – who was trapped in the Ruhr last month with his command?'

Hardt nodded.

'If you recall, he had some three hundred thousand men under his command who hadn't a hope in hell of getting out of the Ruhr Pocket. Hell, we had an army in place on either side of them. Okay, now Model was not about to surrender to us, in spite of his hopeless position. He knew the Russians wanted him as a criminal and that once he had surrendered we, the Americans, would hand him over to their not very tender mercies. So what did he do? The sly bastard ran a crash programme to get every man under his command who was not actually in the firing line equipped with a complete set of release papers, officially separating him from the German Army so that in the end when his men packed up, we had a bunch of civvies on our hands and a runaway Field Marshal, who if we are to believe Eisenhower's intelligence boys has now committed suicide and has been buried at some unmarked spot by his staff officers. You see what I'm getting at son?'

'I think so, sir. You mean we've already gotten our General, who has disappeared and has presumably committed suicide?'

'Exactly. That poor stiff in the garden.'

'And then, sir?'

'We get the Magyars to separate their men from the service toot sweet. After that it's up to them to find civvies and make their way back through the Russian lines to their own country. Or if they like, they can simply cross the front into our territory here, just as any other civvy, regardless of his nationality, can. Well, Hardt,' Patton snapped, obviously very pleased with himself, 'what do you think of it?'

'It's a swell idea, sir,' Hardt replied enthusiastically, although at the back of his mind a nasty little thought was beginning to grow that somehow or other Patton's idea would mean trouble for T-Force. 'But how are you going to let the Hungarians know of your plan?'

'I know what you mean, son. We have no means of communication with them at this moment. And radio is out, even if we had their codes and wavelengths. The Russkis could just pick up the message and then all hell would be loose.' Patton frowned. 'You can bet your sweet life that they are already monitoring Third Army communications.'

Hardt nodded his understanding.

'So this is the deal, son. I want you to take a couple of half-tracks and crew them with the best guys you've got. Don't ask for volunteers,' he added warningly. 'You always get a lemon in a group of volunteers, who has volunteered because he wants to prove something to himself and then cracks up when it comes down to cases.'

Hardt smiled. The remark was typical of Patton. He commanded his army like a corporal commanding an infantry squad; he could never leave the details to his subordinates, but had to plan everything himself.

'Take that Hungarian driver in the Mercedes to guide you to their HQ,' Patton continued. 'When you get there, tell the dead fellow's Chief-of-Staff what I have just told you about separating their men from the service and dispersing the Hungarian Third Army and tell him, too, that as far as our Intelligence can judge they've got about three or four days to do it before the Russians start moving past Prague. That's their deadline. Four days from now. Got it?'

'Got it, sir?'

For a moment there was silence. Somewhere a cock was beginning to crow and in the dark, skeletal trees outside there was the first twittering of birds. Soon it would be first light.

'Something else, Hardt,' Patton broke the silence.

'Sir.'

'You remember that crown he talked about? Well I want it! The Commies are not going to get it. One day there will be a free Hungary again and if I live that long, it will give me the greatest pleasure to hand it back to the Hungarians. Boy, it would make a helluva fine headline. *Hundred Year Old General Hands Back Crown He Stole In The Big War.*' He chucked impishly at his own humour. 'And while we're talking of theft, son, don't forget to bring those silver talers he talked about. You know what I'm gonna do with them?'

'No, sir.'

'I'm gonna have them melted down and use the silver to make a special medal which I'll give to every single soldier in the Third Army. And do you know what I'll call it? I'll call it the HWC.'

'The HWC?' Hardt asked, telling himself

that some times the Old Man really got carried away. God knows how he would cope with the routine boredom of the peacetime Regular Army!

'Yeah, the Hungarian War Chest Medal! It'll be better than most decorations my boys have received. At least if they're hungry, they can hock it for its silver value.' Suddenly Patton's grin vanished. 'But remember this, son, you're on your own on this one. I'll be very frank with you. Ever since that bad business in Sicily in 1943, it has been nip and tuck between me and General Eisenhower. If it ever came out that I had ordered anything like this, he would fire me just like that!' He clicked his thumb and forefinger together and made Hardt start. 'Kay, if it comes out that you have contacted the Hungarians, I shall swear blind that I never gave you the order to do so. I shall sacrifice you – and your Army career will be ruined. You understand that, Hardt?' He looked sternly at Hardt, who was a younger edition of himself, a man who would go far in the Service if he kept his nose clean.

'I understand, sir,' Hardt answered.

'Fine.' Patton rose to his feet and thrust out his beringed hand. 'Good luck, son. I'm depending upon you...'

FOUR

It was dawn now. But no smoke rose from the chimneys of Pilsen's suburbs into the pale sky, undisturbed by the usual pink flickering of the permanent barrage. For this was the first day of peace in Western Europe and the citizens of Pilsen slept late, recovering from the hectic welcome of the night before. Even the dogs were silent.

It was different in the T-Force lines. There, all was hectic activity. The crews of the three half-tracks Hardt had picked for the mission were hurrying about their tasks, while guards posted at both ends of the cobbled streets kept their eyes open for intruders. The crews' bedrolls were dumped so that they would have more room in the vehicles for the cargo they anticipated bringing back with them, K rations loaded for the forty-eight hours Hardt anticipated the trip there and back would take them – and plenty of extra ammunition for the half-tracks' .55 calibre machine guns. For, as Hardt had told van Fleet, his executive officer, half an hour before, 'I know this is the day the Krauts are supposed to surrender in Western Europe at Rheims, Clarry. But I wonder if everybody up there,' he indicated the road to the east, 'knows that.'

'Yes, I agree skipper,' van Fleet had replied, delighted at the prospect of a little excitement again. 'They tell me that this area has a pretty sizeable German minority. There could well be Kraut Werewolves up in the hills.' Instinctively his hand dropped to his knife, his favourite weapon.

'Don't give me any more problems, Clarry,' Hardt had growled surlily. 'Don't you think I've gotten enough headaches as it is?'

Now it was time for Hardt to explain to his men just exactly what their mission was. The T-Force men were the Third Army's élite and Hardt always made a point of explaining the risks they were going to run on their various missions; the little effort invariably paid dividends. 'Red,' he called to his First Sergeant, whose temper was as fiery as his flaming red hair, 'get the guys together for a moment, will you. I want to brief them.'

Big Red straightened up from the grease gun he was reassembling. 'Okay, sir. Now you guys,' he began in his usual bellow.

'Red!' Hardt interrupted him urgently.

'Do you want to wake up the whole goddam neighbourhood?'

'Sorry, sir,' the enormous, suddenly crimson-faced NCO apologised and began once again, lowering his voice to what he thought was a whisper but which to Hardt's pained ears seemed just short of his original bellow.

'Drop what ya doing and haul ya asses over here. The CO wants to talk to you.'

Hardt flashed a quick look at their faces. The outfit had taken a lot of casualties over these last eleven months, but somehow the crew of his own half-track 'Old Baldy' had survived the long haul from Normandy: Dutchie Schulze, the big slow German-American; Triggerman, ex-Mafia soldier, his skinny, olive-skinned face set in its usual aggressive snarl; Wheels, his driver, a dark smear of oil on his face, wiping his dirty hand on cottonwaste – as usual he had been ensuring Old Baldy's engine was in perfect shape; and Limey, T-Force's radio operator, quick, cocky and utterly dependable despite the fact that he had gone over the hill to join T-Force in Africa. They were all there and the sight of their faces gave him confidence that they might well pull off this strangest of all their missions.

Hardt gave them a moment to settle down

and then he began. 'All right, fellers, I want to put you in the big picture–'

'I don't want to see it, sir,' Limey cried, a pair of black silk panties still covering his head, a prize from the night before, carried with him as Big Red had dragged him protesting from the fat Czech blonde's bed, 'I've seen that particular picture before – and it's lousy!'

There was a mumble of tired laughter from the others, heads still heavy with the night's celebrating.

Hardt joined in and told himself the boys were their usual selves. 'Okay, this is the deal. Three hours ago, General Patton gave us a special mission. As soon as we move out of here…' Swiftly he sketched in the details of their task. 'To put it in simple terms,' he concluded, 'we've got to get to those Hungarians before the Russians do.'

'You mean, sir,' Limey said, always quicker off the mark than the rest of T-Force, 'we've got to help to demob a bunch of enemy soldiers before the Russkis, our allies, get their pinkies on them?'

'That's about it, Limey.'

The little radio operator looked at him incredulously. 'Cor ferk a duck! I've been in some bloody mobs in my time, but this is a real old Fred Karno's.'

Hardt did not know what a 'Fred Karno's' was, but he laughed all the same. 'What did you expect Limey? Has T-Force ever had a mission that was easy? They don't call us he Tough Tittie outfit for nothing, you know.' Then he was businesslike. 'Okay fellers, we move out in five minutes. Usual convoy distance. Make as little noise as possible. And remember this.' His eyes narrowed. 'This is supposed to be the first day of the peace, but don't rely on everybody having gotten the message. *Keep your weapons handy!*'

'Comrade General,' the Russian officer with the gold star of a political commissar on his sleeve called urgently from the window.

Ulanov, lying on the rumpled bed in a dirty singlet and shorts, awoke at once. *'Schto?'* he asked in his Vodka-thickened voice. 'What is it, Filov?'

Filov did not turn, but kept his binoculars focused on the road below. 'There is something going on, Comrade General.'

Ulanov thrust in his stainless steel false teeth and swung himself out of the bed. In his bare feet he padded across the floor, kicking an empty vodka bottle out of the way. With the back of a hairy paw he wiped the grey scum from the previous night's drinking orgy from his thick lips and took the glasses from Filov. *'Amerikan'* he commented after a moment's perusal of the three half-tracks crawling slowly through the empty street towards the broad white highway which ran to Prague. 'It could be a routine patrol.'

'But why the Mercedes?' Filov asked, his eyes red-rimed from having to maintain most of the night's watch on the Americans' activities, while the rest of the liaison team had got drunk. 'What do you make of that, Comrade General?'

Ulanov grunted and fiddled with the focus. But it was still not light enough to make out the Mercedes driver's clothing clearly at that distance. One thing was sure, though. The driver was not an American, because he wasn't wearing a helmet, as even the cooks and clerks were forced to do in that pig Patton's Third Army.

'Do you think he is a civilian, Comrade General?'

Ulanov muttered a gross Russian obscenity. 'Who would have the petrol to drive a Mercedes these days after six years of rationing man?' he rapped. 'Only a military man, of course, you idiot!'

'My apologies for my stupidity, Comrade

General,' Filov muttered.

Ulanov did not hear. He was thinking aloud. 'Three American half-tracks and possibly a military vehicle, definitely not American, of unknown origin.' He tapped his steel teeth with a dirty forefinger. 'Now what does that add up to?'

'One thing is certain, Comrade General,' Filov ventured.

'What?'

Filov pointed down below. 'The Americans are going to cross the agreed-on demarcation line. They must be more than three kilometres on the road to Prague now.'

Ulanov absorbed the information and walked thoughtfully across to the big bottle of cheap Cologne. In the Russian fashion he rubbed it on his face in lieu of water and as an afterthought drabbed his hairy armpits with the stuff. Suddenly he made up his mind. 'They're up to something, what I don't know. Later I'll go across to that cowboy Patton's Headquarters and see what I can find out. But for the time being, Filov, send the following message to the *Stavka* 'American vehicles in troop strength are preparing to cross demarcation line this day. Request orders. Ulanov.'

Abruptly Ulanov was very happy. Perhaps

the little incident with the American half-tracks was just the thing he needed to get Eisenhower to sack that pig Patton, even if they had nothing to do with the Paper...

DAY TWO

'The Reichsführer ... is firmly convinced that the Ivans and *Amis* will be fighting each other in less than six months. Then the *Amis* will need us Germans to help them beat the Popovs... In a year the Reich could be back where it was in 1941!'

The Head of Werewolf Kommando Five
to his Group, May 7th, 1945.

ONE

'Amis!'

Carefully Wiebke backed into the cover of the thick firs which crowned the hill, holding on to her white-blonde hair so that it would not be caught by the twigs.

Down below the Mercedes had come to a halt in front of the tree which barred the white highway. Behind it the half-tracks were slowing down, with soldiers springing over the sides, weapons at the ready. Wiebke could see immediately that they were experienced men.

'How many?' the Fat One asked in his slow ponderous manner, the sweat streaming down his gleaming, crimson cheeks, his monstrous chest heaving rapidly, as if he were finding it difficult to breathe in the midday heat.

Carefully Wiebke counted the soldiers crouched on both sides of the road, while a little group of others examined the tree which the *Kommando* had felled across the road only half an hour before. 'Twenty-one

... no,' she corrected herself, 'twenty-three of them, and the one in the Mercedes. A machine gun on each vehicle.'

'I know,' the Fat One commented.

Wiebke waited tensely. Ever since that terrible night two weeks before when the Fat One had felled her while she was gathering wood in the forest with one blow of his fat fist, ripped off her underclothing and raped her with wordless brutality, she had grown very wary of the *Kommandoführer's* unpredictability. Thus she waited for his reaction in silence, though inside her a little voice was crying out frantically that the *Kommando* must act – *soon.*

The Fat One took his time. He always did. It seemed as if it took words longer to penetrate his thick hide than it did with normal people. Yet all the same Wiebke knew that Fat One was capable of swift, savage action, once he had made a decision.

'What are you going to do?' she asked at last, unable to bear the strain of waiting any longer. Already the *Amis* were beginning to attach steel hawsers to the tree, preparatory to attempting to move it with their vehicles.

The Fat One gave her an odd look. She bent back instinctively, fearful for a moment that he was going to strike her, which he did often for reasons known only to himself. Suddenly he shot out a pudgy, sweat-damp hand with amazing speed for such a gross youth. He caught a fat, gleaming May bug in mid-flight. Slowly, almost pleasurably, he crushed it in his fist. He opened his fingers and stared at the sticky mess of blood and crushed matter intently, with the fascination of the overgrown child that he was, but with none of a child's innocence. *'That!'* he said slowly.

Wiebke Bruhns shivered.

Werewolf Kommando Funf was a mixed hunting commando, made up of boys and girls, none of them older than eighteen, but all of them, whatever their age or their sex, fanatical believers in the National Socialist cause. Even in this hour of defeat. From their earliest youth they had been indoctrinated with the Nazi creed, first in the Young Folk, then later in the Hitler Youth and German Maidens. All of them were former youth leaders who had volunteered immediately for the new secret German resistance movement. Himmler had called it to life the previous winter when it had been clear that the Allies would soon begin to cross the Reich's frontiers to the East and West in strength.

All that long hard winter of 1944-1945 they had been trained in the secret Werewolf camps, which had sprung up all over Germany to prepare the young volunteers from the Hitler Youth and Hitler Maidens for their task. The Head of the Werewolf Organisation, *General der SS und Polizei* Prutzmann, had picked them for the job of assassinating the American-appointed Chief-Burgomaster of the first major city to be captured by them in the Reich, Aachen. But that task had been finally given to another group, who had carried it out successfully in March, while they were ordered to infiltrate the Czech border area from which they all came and to establish an organisation there.

Throughout March and April, unknown to the local population, they had established their secret hideouts and arms dumps in the lonely, thickly forested hills, waiting for the arrival of their leader and the orders he would bring with him from Berlin.

He had arrived on the First of April, April Fool's Day. The lean boys and girls, hardened by years of outdoor living and the training of the last few months could hardly believe their eyes when they saw him. *'Grosser Gott!'* Dieter Wagemut, the tall handsome temporary *Führer*, had gasped, as he caught sight of the grossly fat youth, clad in a skimpy suit from which he seemed about to burst at any moment, 'is Prutzmann trying to play an April Fool's trick on us!'

The Fat One, as they had begun to call him immediately, had looked coldly at the tall handsome seventeen year old with his piglike eyes, which seemed hardly to be there they were buried so deep in his glistening face. But he had said nothing save 'authorization' and thrust a paper into the other boy's hand. Then he had sat down on a tree stump and begun to gobble greedily at a thick sausage sandwich, completely oblivious, or so it seemed, of the excited boys and girls crowding round to read the leadership authorization which was signed not only by Prutzmann but also by *Reichsführer* Himmler himself.

'I just can't believe it,' Dieter said finally. He had spun round and stared contemptuously at the flabby youth wolfing down his sandwich, the sweat running down his gleaming crimson face in streams. 'That mass of blubber enjoys the confidence of the *Reichsführer!* They must be crazy in Berlin to send us anyone like that!'

But the hunting commando soon found out that they were not crazy in Berlin. On the very first night he had spent in their forest hideout, he had raped Heidi, at fourteen the youngest member of the *Kommando.* Stark naked, his monstrous body gleaming with sweat, erect organ held out in front of him like a *Schupo's* club, he had waddled into her tent, ripped open her sleeping bag and thrusting her tanned legs apart, had plunged himself cruelly into her virgin body.

Her screams had roused the camp, naturally. Dieter had rushed across. 'In three devils' names, what are you doing, you fat pig?' he had yelled angrily. Slowly, his chest heaving rapidly, the Fat One had risen from the blubbering girl, leaving her on the sleeping bag, blood trickling down her inner thighs, surmounted with the faint puff of girlish pubic hair. 'I've done it!' he grunted.

'You raped her by God!' Dieter cried. 'Don't you understand?' Besides himself with rage, he rushed at the Fat One.

The gross youth moved with amazing speed. His fat paw clubbed in a fist caught Dieter to the right of his neck. He howled with pain and doubled up. The Fat One's pudgy knee rammed into Dieter's crotch. He flew back onto the grass, his mouth full of vomit, making strange little whimpering noises, as he rolled from side to side, knees clenched under his chin in unbearable agony. The Fat One had not even looked down as he stepped over the other boy and waddled back to his own tent, his monstrous belly trembling like a plate of jelly.

Thereafter he had taken every female member of the *Kommando* when and where it pleased him to do so. But although they feared the Fat One, they also admired him. He was the born leader and organiser. In his first week he had organised a raid which had wiped out a fifty-strong group of Czech Underground men who had been attempting to snipe the retreating German troops on the road from Prague to Pilsen. A week later, he had publicly shot the burgomaster of a nearby hamlet, which housed only Germans, because he had told the farmers that they should no longer supply the Werewolves with food; the war was lost. Two days after that he had strung up three stragglers from a *Luftwaffe* unit: they had thrown away their weapons and he left them dangling from telegraph posts with the crude sign attached to their skinny dead chests. *WE RAN AWAY. THIS WAS OUR REWARD!* There were fewer stragglers from the retreating German armies after that.

But now the first Americans were here. Soon the Russians would arrive in this part of Czechoslovakia too. And the fifty young people, assembled in the glade at the top of the hill, waiting expectantly for the Fat One's orders, knew that their real job, the one they had been trained for, was about to begin.

The Fat One finished munching his apple, as if he had all the time in the world, picked his front teeth with a forefinger that was thick as a sausage, and finally broke his long silence. 'We Germans talk too much,' he announced in his high-pitched voice. 'It's a fault. But I must explain in a little detail what our assignment here really is. It is not to frighten a few traitors or kill a handful of those Slav pigs. No.' He wiped away the beads of sweat which were dripping from the end of his big fleshy nose. 'The *Reichsführer* had something else in mind for *Werewolf Kommando Funf.* He is firmly convinced that the Ivans and the *Amis* will be fighting each other in less than six months. Then the *Amis* will need us Germans to help them beat the Popovs. We have the men, the know-how, the courage. In a year the Reich could be back where it was in 1941.'

The eyes of his listeners gleamed with new hope. In spite of their fanaticism, they could not blind themselves to the fact that the *Wehrmacht* had been badly beaten in the field. Now the Fat One's coarsely grunted words were like music to their ears.

'But the *Reichsführer* knows that time is running out for the Reich. Time is on the side of our enemies. Soon our armies will be demobilised or behind barbed wire in enemy concentration camps. We must have the Ivans and *Amis* fighting each other soon. That is our assignment – to help that inevitable confrontation along. Those *Amis* half-tracks down there will be our start.'

'How do you mean?' Wiebke asked hesitantly.

The Fat One grunted and reached into his pocket. He pulled out a pistol of an unfamiliar make and tossed it across to her. She caught it easily and looked down at the Cyrillic script on the butt. 'Russian?'

Again the Fat One grunted and fumbled in his pocket. He brought out a thin wad of dark coloured passes, with a worn red star stamped on the front. 'Red Army military identification documents,' he announced.

'But I don't understand,' Dieter Wagemut said. 'The pistol and the passes – what have they got to do with those *Amis* down there and the start of a new war?'

The Fat One grinned, his eyes nearly disappearing in folds of fat. 'Those *Amis* are going to meet with a nasty accident soon and when their people come to search for them, they're going to find those passes and pistol near the bodies. Now do you understand?'

Dieter whistled softly through his teeth. 'You mean the *Amis* will conclude that ... that the Popovs did it?'

'Brilliant, Dieter, brilliant,' the Fat One said contemptuously.

Dieter Wagemut flushed hotly, but he said nothing.

'All right, this is what you will do. It'll take the *Amis* another thirty minutes to clear that tree. By that time I want another felled two kilometres further up the road where it goes through the gorge. This time the *Kommando* will be waiting for them to ensure that they have their little accident. All right, don't just stand there. Air your asses!'

As the *Kommando* hurried into the trees to carry out his orders, the Fat One pulled another apple out of his pocket and bit into it. Obviously enjoying it, he followed them leisurely, as if he were taking a comfortable stroll through the forest.

TWO

'Phew!' Hardt breathed out hard and wiped the beads of sweat from his forehead, as the combined efforts of the three half-tracks finally succeeded in moving the fallen oak sufficiently to allow the little convoy to edge its way by, without going into the deep drainage ditch at the left side of the road. 'Brother, I hope we're not going to run into too many of these bastards – we'll never make it to the Hungarians.'

The watching Hungarian Colonel who had driven Colonel-General Jerzy to his death at Patton's HQ nodded. 'We waste much time – much time,' he said gravely.

'I don't know about that,' van Fleet said and rubbed his reddened hands still smarting from the effort of pushing the tree trunk, 'but it sure spoiled my manicure.'

Hardt laughed softly, but there was no answering warmth in his eyes. He was worried.

'Are you thinking the same as me, sir?' Limey asked as van Fleet and the Hungarian began to walk back to their own vehicles, ready to move on again.

'What do you mean?'

'Well, sir, what puzzles me is who put that bloody thing there in the first place?'

'Yeah, Limey, I was kinda thinking on those lines myself a minute ago.'

'Yer, the Jerries have passed through here. They didn't put it there. You can see from the stump that it has been freshly felled.'

'Agreed.'

'The Czechs are not interested in stopping anybody. They're too busy whooping it up at the moment.'

Hardt nodded.

'And the Russkis are nowhere in sight. So if it wasn't any one of them, who soddingly well was it, eh, sir? That's what I'd like to know.'

Hardt remained silent for a moment. He stared up at the fir-capped hilltops, silent, peaceful, yet somehow heavy with an unknown menace. In spite of the heat of the afternoon, he shivered, feeling a cold finger of fear trace its way down the small of his back.

'Anything up, sir?'

Hardt forced himself to grin. 'No, I guess a ghost must have walked over my grave, that's all.'

'Don't say things like that, sir!' Limey objected. 'Remember, sir, this is peacetime, you don't talk about graves in peacetime.'

'No, Limey, I don't suppose you do,' Hardt replied thoughtfully, but his voice carried no conviction.

Now the spring sun was at its zenith: a ball of golden fire in a burning blue sky. Above the spiked outline of the firs marching over the hills on both sides of the white road the heat haze rippled in trembling lines. With the back of his olive-drab shirt wet and black with sweat, Wheels began to drive Old Baldy up the steep incline which snaked its way to the pass through the hills. Behind Old Baldy, van Fleet followed in the second half-track, then came the Hungarian in the Mercedes, with Sergeant Holman in the third half-track bringing up the rear. Hardt had ordered the formation so that he had armour to the front and rear, covering the Hungarian's soft vehicle. Since they had encountered the first obstacle he was not going to take any more chances.

Now as Old Baldy came ever closer to the top of the pass, he scanned the ground ahead anxiously, automatically noting the danger points – the narrowness of the road, the steep slopes on both sides of the cut, the dense fir forest which could hide a whole regiment of troops easily.

'Worried, sir?' Big Red growled, following the direction of his gaze, knowing that the CO had changed the formation of the convoy for one purpose only – protection.

'I guess so, Red. This is the sort of place we could get goosed very easily.'

'Yeah. But by who, sir?'

'I wish I knew, Red, it would help. All I know is that it was no goddam woodpecker that laid that log across the highway back there.'

'You can say that again, sir,' Big Red answered. 'But I think we're ready for anybody who tries to come it tough with us.' He gave a jerk of his head at the rest of the crew, each one of them in his position: Triggerman crouched by the 50 calibre machine-gun; Limey behind his radio ready to relay any order to the other half-tracks immediately; while Dutchie Schulze peered over the left side of the half-track, grease gun at the alert.

'Good, Red,' Hardt nodded his approval. 'Okay, you take the right hand side and I'll cover the front from the cab here. And

Wheels,' he spoke to the driver, 'if we come to an obstacle, it'll be up to you to get us through.'

'Sure, sir,' the little ex-cabbie grunted. 'Leave it to me. Me and Old Baldy'll swing it okay.'

Surprisingly enough, nothing happened. They reached the top of the pass without incident. As they began to breast the hill prior to descending into the green lush valley below, Hardt breathed a sigh of relief and lowered his grease gun. 'I must be getting old, Red, but I thought we were in–'

The words froze on his lips. Fifty feet below the top of the pass a great tree blocked the road, its foliage rising up at least seven feet and blotting out everything beyond.

'Christ on a crutch!' Big Red groaned, 'they did it after all!'

Cautiously Wheels eased his foot off the accelerator. Ahead all was silent. Nothing moved, save the leaves of the tree, stirred by the faint hot wind that came from the valley below.

Hardt licked his dry lips. He had to make a decision. Soon! He had only a matter of moments before the trouble started – and start it would. Wildly he cast about for some way out of the trap.

To the right the hill fell off from the shoulder. A sheer drop through stunted scrub and naked rock of perhaps three hundred feet. That was out. His gaze flashed to the left of the blocked road.

The Czech engineers, or whoever had built the road, had smoothed away the rock there to a height of about twelve feet in an arching half-tunnel effect that had left a rock overhang probably with the intention of keeping the winter snow up in the firs and preventing it from falling directly onto the road. But they hadn't done too good a job of cleaning up the rock. It was chipped, creviced in spots, with loose boulders and chippings lying at its base. By American engineering standards it was a pretty dirty piece of work. But at that moment, as the second half-track breasted the hill, it offered the only hope that Hardt could discover of getting out of the mess they were going to be in any moment now.

'Wheels,' he yelled, 'to the left!'

'Holy cow,' Wheels cried, 'not up there!'

'It's our only chance. Limey, radio the others to follow us.' Without waiting for Wheels to protest further, he clambered over him and swung himself over the side of the half-track. Holding on by one arm, he cried, 'Okay, Wheels, let 'em roll! ... and hold tight the rest of you guys!'

Dutchie crossed himself hastily and grabbed for the nearest stanchion. The rest did the same, as Wheels gingerly eased the six ton half-track on the shoulder of the road. It lurched alarmingly. 'Come on ... for Chrissake, come on, Wheels!' Hardt ordered. 'We'll do it!'

With a lurch the half-track ground up the slope. Abruptly it was tilting at a forty-five degree angle. Grimly Hardt held on with all his strength. If the tracks started sliding now, they would overturn and that would be that. There was no denying that. Wheels shook his head to drive away the sweat-beads which threatened to blind him. In his hands the steering wheel quivered frantically.

'Don't let go!' Hardt yelled frantically.

Wheels muttered an obscenity. The muscles standing out against his sweat-blackened shirt, he held onto the wildly trembling wheel desperately.

They were almost up to the tree now. Soon the shooting would start. But that prospect didn't worry Hardt. His sole concern was to get the half-track along that rocky slope. Behind them, van Fleet's half-track began the same trick. Hardt, his whole attention concentrated on the way ahead, could hear the rattle of shifting jerry cans and equipment as van Fleet's vehicle hit the slope. But he didn't look back. He couldn't.

The boughs of the felled tree scraped against the half-track's metal sides. In that same instant, the tracks began to slip. With a gasp of alarm, Hardt could feel the half-track start to slide. *'Hit the gas, Wheels!'* he cried frantically, *'GAS!'*

Wheels spun the steering wheel to the left and simultaneously put his foot down on the accelerator hard. Nothing happened! The half-track started to swing downwards by the tail.

'Everyone over to the left!' Hardt ordered. *'QUICK!'*

Desperately the other three men scrambled to the left side of the half-track, leaning their bodies far out like a bobsleigh team making a steep curve while Wheels, cursing crazily, fought the sliding tracks. Then suddenly the half-track was moving forward again. Green foliage blinded them. Hardt ducked hastily. A twig snapped back and hit him across the face like the lash from a whip. He didn't even feel it. They had done it – they had done it! A moment later, Wheels twisted the wheel to the right. With a crash the six ton vehicle hit the road again, the tree behind it.

'Wheels, you horrible, short-assed bastard, you did ... did it!' Big Red cried exuberantly and slapped a sweat-soaked Wheels across the back with his mighty paw.

But there was no time for congratulations now. The first shot of the ambush came, as Hardt knew it must come. The dry flat crack of a rifle sounded like a twig being snapped underfoot. Lead whined off the side of Old Baldy.

As van Fleet's half-track nosed its way cautiously by the tree, its tail sliding to the right, scattering pebbles and chippings everywhere, the firs above them erupted with small arms fire. A kid in short black pants came half-running, half-falling down the steep slope. Hardt fired instinctively. The kid's head shattered in a spray of red vapour. The headless body slithered to a stop against a tree. Another kid came out of the trees, a Schmeisser clutched to his side. With the 50 calibre, Triggerman fired a rapid burst. Tracer zig-zagged into the trees. *'Jesus H!'* he gasped suddenly and took his finger off the trigger, as if the metal were red-hot. As the kid went down, almost sawn in half by the burst, her skirt fluttered up to reveal the simple white school-girl knickers underneath. 'It's a dame!'

But Hardt had no time to worry about the identity or sex of their attackers. As Wheels eased the half-track a little way down the slope to leave room for the others, his sole concern was that his remaining two vehicles should make it past the barrier.

Now it was the Hungarian's turn. Hardt could see the big automobile's squat hood crushing down the foliage of the tree as it began the passage. 'Come on, come on!' he heard himself calling, oblivious of the lead pattering against the half-tracks metal sides like heavy tropical rain. 'Make it, you Honky bastard – *make it!*'

Grimly the middle-aged Hungarian fought the wheel. Once the Mercedes started to slip. He caught it just in time. Hardt could see his white strained face quite clearly as he wrenched the wheel from side to side, desperately trying to keep the Mercedes from overturning. He was nearly through now. Hardt gulped with relief. The Hungarian was going to make it! 'Red,' he yelled, 'be ready to give him covering fire when he comes out from beyond the tree!'

'Roger, sir!'

And then it happened. A terrible jarring

rocked the car. Its nose dipped. There was the sound of wrenching metal. Its back slithered round in a flurry of white dust. The wheels raced. But the panic-stricken Hungarian could no longer hold it. In wide-eyed horror Hardt watched as it slid to rest on the side of the tree, wheels spinning impotently.

It was the moment their unknown attackers had been waiting for. They concentrated all their fire on the trapped vehicle. The front tyre exploded with the roar of 75mm shells. An instant later the windscreen shattered into a spider's web of broken glass. Hardt caught one last glimpse of the Hungarian slumping forward over the wheel and the Mercedes' horn began to sound as he slumped over it, dead or unconscious.

Hardt knew that there was no hope for the third half-track. It would never be able to pass the wrecked Mercedes. 'Limey, radio Holman to back off – head for Pilsen,' he yelled urgently. 'You, Wheels, step on the gas! Let's get the hell outa here before it's too late!'

Wheels needed no urging. He pressed his foot down to the floor. The half-track shot forward. At seventy miles an hour, it roared down the road from the pass, with van Fleet's driver trying to keep up as best he could, pursued by the sound of the horn wailing like an abandoned child for its lost mother...

THREE

The Fat One kicked the American slumped in the middle of the road like a broken puppet. The man did not move.

'Dead,' Dieter said, still panting with the excitement of his first real engagement.

'Hm,' the Fat One grunted. He was angry at the failure of his plan. The *Amis* in the third half-track, who had backed off after the Mercedes had failed to get past the tree barrier would surely report that their attackers were not Russians. In a black mood he walked over to the wrecked car.

The Hungarian was unconscious, but still alive. One leg doubled underneath him at an unnatural angle, he lay over the wheel with the two halves of his broken dentures lying on the dashboard grinning up at him.

'Stop that shitty horn!' the Fat One commanded.

Dieter reached inside the shattered mess

and lifted the Hungarian by his blood-wet grey hair, pulled him away from the wheel. With his other hand he turned off the ignition. The horn stopped abruptly.

'Gott sei dank!' the Fat One breathed and wiped his sweat-lathered face. 'That racket was enough to drive anybody mad.'

'We've suffered three cas–' Wiebke began, as she thrust her way through the tree's shattered foliage.

The Fat One held up his pudgy hand for silence. The words froze on her lips and there was no sound save that of the wind and the soft moans of the fifteen year old boy dying in the ditch on the other side of the tree. Curiously the Fat One stared down at the unconscious Mercedes driver, whose breath was coming in short, shallow gasps. 'You,' he indicated Dieter, 'you come from these parts, what do you make of him? Is that Czech uniform?'

'No, Czech uniform is a lighter colour and his has a crown, indicating a monarchy–'

'Shut up, arsehole,' the Fat One rapped irritably. 'I don't want a lecture. What uniform is it?'

'I know,' Wiebke ventured hesitantly.

'Well?'

'It's Hungarian – the Royal Hungarian

Army. I was in Budapest in forty-three with my father. I remember it from there.'

The Fat One sucked his sensual bottom lip like a petulant child. What in three devils' names was a Hungarian officer doing with American soldiers in the middle of the God-forsaken Czech countryside? And by the look of the car and his gold braid, an important Hungarian to boot.

'What do you make of it?' Wiebke asked, when the Fat One did not speak again. 'A Hungarian and no Hungarian troops around here anywhere, as we know.'

The Fat One didn't answer her question. Instead he bent down and slapped the Hungarian's face. Once, twice, three times. The Hungarian groaned, but didn't open his eyes. The Fat One hit him again. His eyelids flickered and his eyes opened slowly. He said something in a language they did not understand. The Fat One hit him again. 'Speak German,' he ordered. 'All you comic opera Central European soldiers speak it.'

'Are you German?' the Hungarian asked weakly.

'No, I'm Santa Claus,' the Fat One answered contemptuously. 'You, who are you and what are you doing here with the *Amis?*'

'My name is Madgaleny. I am a Colonel in

the Hungarian Army,' the Hungarian said in good German.

'And what are you doing here?'

'Water!'

'I asked you a question. Answer it.' The Fat One hit the Hungarian in the face again. He groaned and let his head fall to the seat once more.

'Enough of this,' the Fat One snapped, 'get him out of that car. I'll soon get the bastard to confess.' Suddenly he had forgotten the failure of their first attack on the *Amis*. His curiosity was aroused. Now he felt he was on to something.

'This might not be the most elegant of devices,' the Fat One announced, when the rest of the *Kommando* had finished trussing the Hungarians as he'd ordered. 'But it is guaranteed to make even an Egyptian mummy confess.' He chuckled throatily at his own humour, his jowls wobbling violently.

The Hungarian swallowed and said nothing, but his yellow eyes revealed eloquently just how afraid he was. They had tied him down with his wrists attached securely to a log that had been strapped to his back. Now he swayed there at the edge of the little mountain stream, wondering yet already knowing what was going to happen to him.

The Fat One nodded to Dieter. The handsome young Hitler Youth leader stuck out his foot. The next instant the Fat One struck the helpless Hungarian a hard blow on the chest. He tumbled backwards and fell onto the dry grass. 'What are you going to do?' he quavered fearfully.

The Fat One did not answer. Instead he snapped his thumb and forefinger together imperiously. Wiebke handed him the thick towel. Carefully the Fat One bent with a grunt at the effort and dipped the towel in the water until it was soaked. Satisfied, he straightened up again and looked down at the Hungarian. 'Are you going to sing?'

The Hungarian did not trust himself to speak. Mutely he shook his head.

The Fat One did not hesitate. He flung the soaked towel across the trussed-up man's face. The Hungarian tried to rise and shake it off. Lazily the Fat One put his boot in his mouth and shoved him down again. 'Canteen,' he ordered.

Dieter handed him the water canteen. Slowly and deliberately savouring the action, as if he were enjoying it, the Fat One started to pour more water into the towel which now clung to the Hungarian's face like a mask.

Desperately the Hungarian writhed from side to side, trying to blow out the water which was now seeping through the material into his mouth and nostrils. 'If you're not careful,' he gasped frantically, 'you're going to choke me!'

'Exactly,' the Fat One said pleasurably. 'Exactly!' He continued pouring.

'It is a very simple but effective torture,' the Fat One lectured the horrified boys and girls watching the Hungarian's wild struggles on the grass. 'The moisture keeps the towel in place. Every time he breathes, he draws the material ever more tightly to his face. Now, if I stop wetting the towel like this,' he suited his actions to his words and the Hungarian stopped struggling, 'he can breathe relatively well. But as soon as I start pouring again,' he began to let the water drop from the canteen once more, 'each successive breath provides less and less oxygen for his lungs. Soon he will black out. When he comes to–'

To his right, one of the girls screamed and turned away, her hands covering her face.

'Stupid cow!' the Fat One snapped angrily. 'I will deal with you later – I'll have the knickers off you this night for that!'

He turned his attention to his victim.

'Well, as I was saying, when he comes to he will think it is all over. But it isn't. He does not know *der Dicker.* I shall continue until he either talks or dies.'

Twice the Hungarian escaped into the delicious oblivion of unconsciousness, and twice when he thought it was all over, the Fat One started all over again, as if he had all the time in the world. The third time he came to with more difficulty, to find that the Fat One was applying the end of a lighted cigar to the back of his hands to bring him round. His little piglike eyes were full of unconcealed pleasure.

'Oh, my God, have you no mercy,' he groaned weakly.

Almost solemnly the Fat One shook his head and applied the cigar once again.

The Hungarian shrieked and broke, 'All right ... all right!' he gasped, 'I'll talk...'

They had given him a drink of local plum brandy, supplied under pressure by the local farmers, although none of them drank. Now he began to talk. He explained how Colonel-General Jerzy had attempted to surrender his Army to the Americans and failed; but how, after his suicide, the American General Patton had decided to send a mission to the

Hungarians. The mission would order the Hungarians to demobilise themselves before the Russians came and also return to Patton's HQ with 'certain items'.

'What items?' the Fat One asked, munching at yet another apple thoughtfully.

'The War Chest of the Third Hungarian Army, the Crown of St Stephan and,' the Hungarian hesitated, 'certain documents.'

'What documents?'

Still the Hungarian hesitated.

The Fat One's curiosity was aroused. Already a vague plan was beginning to form at the back of his mind. He paused in the middle of a greedy bite, his mouth full of apple. 'You don't want the towel again, do you?' he said threateningly.

The Hungarian's left cheek twitched violently. For a moment the Fat One thought the soldier was going to break down and cry. 'No, no, please not that!' the Hungarian held up his hands protectively, as if to ward him off, 'I'll talk.'

'Naturally you will,' the Fat One said easily and commenced munching his apple again.

'You see in the summer of 1944 there were those around Admiral Horthy, the Regent of Hungary, who thought it was time to break the alliance with you Germans and attempt to make peace with the Russians before it was too late. In particular Miklos – *Mickey*, as they called him – the son of the Admiral, started making overtures to the Russians without his father's knowledge.'

'Yes, that was before our Skorzeny rolled him up in a carpet and spirited him out of the palace in Budapest right under the eyes of his guards. The Traitor,' Dieter Wagemut said. 'If it hadn't been for Skorzeny you Hungarians would have–'

'*Schnauze*,' the Fat One silenced him brutally. 'Who told you to interfere, you asparagus Tarzan!'

The Hungarian looked from the one boy to the other, wondering whether he should go on. A kick in the ribs from the Fat One told him he should. 'Twice the young Horthy met the Russian Foreign Minister Molotov,' he continued hastily, 'to find out what the Russian conditions would be if we Hungarians decided to make a separate peace with them. Now a lot of people thought Mickey was a playboy – the fast cars, the mistresses, the nightclubs, the uniforms – but all the same he had his father's head on his shoulders. He was no fool. To protect himself, he made certain provisions. He asked for and received,' the Hungarian licked his blood-scummed lips, 'the Molotov Paper.'

'The what?'

Hesitantly the Hungarian began to explain. When he was finished, the Fat One sat in silence for a very long time, while the rest of the *Kommando,* squatting in the long hot grass of the hilltop, waited for his reaction. There was no sound save the drip-drip of water from the Mercedes' fractured radiator.

Finally the Fat One broke the long silence. 'Folk Comrades,' he announced with surprising formality, 'I think that Werewolf Commando Five must ensure that the *Amis* convey the Molotov Paper to that General of theirs, eh.' He grinned suddenly. 'I think we'll have that war yet.' Then as an afterthought, he jerked a thumb at the Hungarian and barked at Dieter, 'Get rid of that pig, will you, Wagemut?'

FOUR

'The Hungarians were here, Filov,' Ulanov snapped, throwing off his hat as he entered the room. 'Pass me the vodka.'

The Political Commissar passed him the

bottle. Ulanov sprinkled a generous portion of salt onto the V of skin made by his outstretched forefinger and thumb, licked off the salt in one go and then took a generous swig of the fiery liquid straight from the bottle. He belched, his eyes sparkling suddenly. '*Brr*, that's better!' he said thickly.

'The Hungarians?' the Political Commissar reminded him. The General ripped open the front of his tunic to reveal a dirty white shirt, ragged at the collar. From the shirt pocket he took a leather wallet and tossed it to the other man. 'One of our people who is acting as a cleaner at that pig Patton's HQ found it in a bathroom. I can't read the lingo, but it's Magyar all right.'

He stumped across the room and stared out of the window at the sun setting over the Czech city, while Filov opened the wallet and took out the picture. It showed an elderly man in uniform, complete with full medals and sword, posed with a silver-haired woman and two young, grinning boys in uniform, who looked as if they might have just graduated from the officers' academy. Curiously Filov turned it over and noted the date '2.1.45'. 'You saw the date, Comrade General?' he asked.

Ulanov swung round, his face flushed with

the heat and the vodka. 'I saw it,' he answered grimly.

'It indicates–'

'I know what it indicates, man,' Ulanov interrupted. 'It indicates that the Hungarians have been here recently to contact the Americans. Now we know where that Mercedes came from this morning. It came from the Third Hungarian Army. It is obvious that they have the Paper.'

'Do you think the Americans know?'

'I don't know, Filov. It is immaterial anyway. Even if they do, they haven't got it yet. But if they ever do, you can imagine what that creature Patton would do with it! That man hates us Russians like the plague – he would ensure that its contents were blazoned across every decadent capitalist rag in the West. And at the moment, Comrade Stalin cannot afford to have that happen. Later we shall be able to deal with pigs. But now, no!' He went over to the bottle and repeated the procedure, while Filov waited patiently for his decision.

It came quickly enough. 'We will radio the *Stavka* of our findings here and suggest the Third Hungarian Army must be taken or eliminated before the Americans reach them, or there will be all hell to pay. Make the message top priority. General officer's eyes only. Now Filov get on with it and in the name of the Holy Mother of Kazan, be careful. We don't want the Americans picking it up.'

Filov spat on the bottle-littered dirty floor contemptuously. 'The Americans would never break our code, Comrade General, if they tried from now to the end of the world!'

But there Filov was wrong. The interception of Ulanov's message and its decoding took exactly two hours. Just before dusk it was picked up at a remote English country house in the Home Counties. The elderly ex-Dons, mathematicians, former cross-word experts and the rest of that strange team of men and women who, between croquet sessions and amateur dramatic evenings, had provided Churchill with the most intimate secrets of the Third Reich throughout the war and who were now turning their hands to the secrets of the potential new enemy from the East, went at it like a terrier after a rat. Within the hour they had broken it with the aid of their machine, against which no code was proof. Thirty minutes later it was re-encoded and winging its way over the air to the Ultra

Organisation attached to General Bradley's HQ. Major Flint received it personally from the British and took it to Patton immediately he had finished supper.

'Well, Black Market?' Patton asked, using Flint's code-name, 'haven't seen you for a few days. What are you SIS people doing these days with no enemy signal traffic to listen to?'

'This, sir!' the sharp young major said, thrusting the intercept flimsy into Patton's surprised hands. 'It's marked *sekretiski*, which is Russian for "secret". And,' he paused slightly before the punchline, 'it originated here in Pilsen.'

Patton took the cigar out of his mouth. 'You mean Ulanov?'

Black Market nodded.

'Here, give it here.'

Swiftly Patton put on his steel-rimmed GI glasses and stared down at the piece of paper. 'Americans attempting to contact Third Hungarian Army,' he read. 'Position estimated between Prague and Pilsen. Believe possess Molotov Paper. Recommend capture or elimination before Americans can contact.'

Slowly Patton put down the paper and, taking off his glasses, looked hard at Flint.

'What do you make of it, Black Market?'

'Not much to be honest, sir!'

'But what in hell's name has Molotov got to do with the Third Hungarian Army?' Patton mused aloud.

Flint shrugged. 'Search me, sir.'

Patton made a decision. 'Get me Koch, will you, Black Market.'

Ten minutes later the three of them, Patton, Black Market, and Colonel Koch, Patton's tubby, professional looking Chief-of-Intelligence, were closeted in the General's office, bourbon in hand, pondering the message. Outside the celebration bonfires turned night into day, casting their shadows in grotesque flickering magnification on the walls.

'Let us establish what we *do* know,' Koch began in that systematic manner of his. 'One, the Russians have tumbled to the fact that the Hungarians were here.'

'Yes,' Patton said, a little unhappily.

'Two. They know that we are attempting to contact the Hungarians by means of Major Hardt's T-Force.'

Patton's frown deepened, as if he were already visualizing the final interview with Eisenhower that would surely take place if what he had done ever came into the open.

But he said nothing.

'Three.' Koch ticked off the point on his fingers. 'It is obvious from the message's priority and the fact it is intended for general officer's eyes only that the Russians are greatly interested in not having that contact made.' He paused and let his words sink in. 'The question is now, *why* they don't want that link-up to be made and *why* they would go to such lengths to prevent it?'

Patton's face lit up. 'Of course! Under normal circumstances, Antonov, the Red Army's Chief-of-Staff, could contact Ike and tell him what I'm up to. Ike would fall on top of me like a brick shithouse and the matter would be solved.'

Colonel Koch pursed his lips primly at Patton's choice of phrase; the Commanding General's language could still shock him although he had served with him a couple of years now. 'Exactly, sir. No, there is more to it.'

'Because of this Molotov business, Colonel?' Flint ventured.

'Right, Major. What has the Soviet Foreign Minister got to do with a minor Hungarian Army on the run? And why must that Army be eliminated or captured before we can link up with it? And what is the

Molotov Paper?...' He shrugged slightly, as if it were all a little too much for him at this time of night. 'A lot of questions and few answers, General.'

Patton did not answer. Instead he sat there silently, puffing stolidly at his big cigar. From far-off there came the throaty sound of one of the local brass bands playing a polka. Idly Patton thought he had not been to a dance since Pearl Harbour; it seemed an age ago. With sudden irritation he dismissed the thought from his mind. There was still a war being fought in Europe, whatever those dancing Czechs, celebrating the day of victory out there, thought to the contrary: a new secret war, which would be fought remorselessly and mercilessly in the shadows and in the end would be more terrible than the shooting war.

'All right,' he said finally, 'we're fighting this one in the dark, fellows. But by God, I'm not going to let the Russians get away with it without a fight. Unfortunately I put T-Force on the strictest radio silence during this operation for obvious reasons. Okay, we can't reach them by radio. But we can do it by air. Oscar,' he turned to Koch, 'as soon as it's dawn, I want an L-5 up, looking for them. They can pass onto him what the

Russians are up to with the Eureka.'

Colonel Koch nodded his understanding, realising that Patton was prepared to risk the top secret ground-to-air radio device in order to help Hardt. It was a sign that the Old Man had thrown off his black mood of the last thirty-six hours; he had gotten the bit between his teeth again. He was raring for a fight, even if it were against their erstwhile allies, the Russians. 'And have you any idea where the pilot might find T-Force, sir?' he asked quietly.

Koch's question hit home. 'Oscar,' Patton cried angrily, 'must you always ask such goddam foolish questions? How the hell would I know where they are! As of this morning T-Force might as well have vanished from the face of the earth...'

FIVE

At that particular moment, a harassed, red-faced Major Hardt, surrounded by giggling young blonde women in various stages of undress, felt a little as if he had indeed been abruptly transported into another world.

Half an hour before, the blood red ball of the sun had finally vanished behind the hills and he had realised it was time that he got his two half-tracks off the road. There they were at the mercy of any teenage Werewolf armed with a bazooka: easy meat for the most inexperienced Hitler Youth. He started to search for a place for the night.

They passed through two Czech hamlets. The houses were in darkness and silent, yet he sensed there were frightened men and women pressed close to the other side of the wooden shutters listening tensely to each sound, crossing themselves with relief when the noise of the engines passed away. Here in this no-man's land between the Russians and the Americans, they were at the mercy of deserters, stragglers, the riff-raff of half a dozen defeated armies. He knew that and didn't blame them for their caution. All the same he was longing for a bite to eat and a bed for the night; and he knew that his men were probably feeling exactly the same. It had been a very long day.

Just when he had been about to give up the search for a place to bed down for the night and was about to order his men to make a laager at the roadside, they had spotted the house. A large gabled structure, set a quarter of a mile or so from the road along a dirt track. By the light of the moon, he could see that all its lower windows were tightly shuttered, just as those in the hamlets had been; but there were faint yellow lights in the upstairs windows – probably candles, he guessed – which indicated the lonely house was occupied. He had made a decision. While the two half-tracks had taken cover, he had detailed Dutchie, Trigger and Limey to make a reconnaissance of the lonely country house.

They had returned half an hour later, their faces glowing, their eyes sparkling excitedly in the rays of the moon, all weariness vanished now.

'Well?' Hardt had demanded.

'Judies, sir!' Limey had responded eagerly. 'Bints, dames, scores of 'em. Lovely grub. A real knocking shop if I ever did see one – and I've seen plenty!'

'What did you say?' Hardt had asked in open-mouthed bewilderment at the excited flow of words.

'He means a cathouse, sir,' Triggerman had snarled. 'These goddam foreigners can't even speak American!'

'No, sir, it isn't a – whorehouse,' Dutchie interrupted in his usual earnest manner. 'It's what the Krauts call a *Lebensbornheim.*'

'What's that, Dutchie?'

'That's what the Krauts call the place where selected dames are brought together with selected servicemen, mostly SS,' he had explained, 'so that they can breed big, blond baby boys. For the Führer that is. They don't have to get married, even if they get in the family way.'

'Brother,' Big Red had sighed. 'We must have gotten into the wrong goddam army, fellers!'

They had all laughed and Limey had pawed the ground with his right foot like an impatient stallion, exclaiming, 'Come on, let's get at it – all that lovely grub!'

And he had been right. The girls were lovely in a cold blonde Nordic manner. But there was nothing cold about their reception. They were pathetically grateful for the T-Force's men's presence. As they crowded into the dark hallway the girls surrounded the weary GIs, giggling and laughing, explaining excitedly in a mixture of German, Czech and broken English that they were scared of a Cossack attack. Apparently the renegade Cossacks, who had once fought for the Germans, were now living as bandits in the hills, pillaging, plundering and raping the helpless civilian populace, trying to forget the inevitable – the day when the Red Army would come for them in an orgy of drinking and women.

'Vergewaltigung, die vergewaltigen alles zwischen zwölf und sechszig!' a big blonde, whose massive bosom seemed about to burst out of her too tight silk blouse at any moment, cried excitedly. And she made her meaning quite clear with an obscene gesture of her thumb and forefinger.

'Rape – they rape everything between twelve and sixty,' Dutchie interpreted unnecessarily.

Limey's eyes gleamed wickedly. 'I could do with a little bit of the other myself,' he announced sotto voce. 'The old five against one is getting a bit much. My right hand is going to drop off if I do it much longer.'

They all laughed at the little Cockney's undisguised lechery, even the blondes, who probably hadn't even understood a word of what he had said. But Hardt forced a solemn face and snapped. 'Okay, Limey, knock it off. We're on a mission, remember.'

'I'd rather fuck than fight, sir,' Limey quipped.

Hardt ignored him. 'Now get this the lot of you,' he rasped, 'and you can translate into German, Dutchie, for the benefit of the women. The dames are off-limits. They're all German, I guess, but even if they aren't, I'm declaring them German here and now. And for German women, the non-fraternization ban applies, even if we are here in Czechoslovakia.'

Some of the women giggled when Dutchie had finished translating Hardt's words and he felt himself flushing. He hurried on. 'Now when I dismiss you, you guys can cook your chow. After that I want you to hit the sack, is that understood?'

There was a half-hearted murmur of understanding.

'You'll make out the sentry detail for the night, Red.'

'Yessir,' the big NCO, his face crimson with confusion, took his eyes off the big blonde in the too tight blouse who was ogling him with undisguised invitation.

'And you Dutchie–' he turned to the German-American.

'Sir?'

'I want you to tell the women that they will be confined to the top floor. We'll protect them from the Cossacks, you can tell them!' He stared grimly at a grinning Limey and gave him a warning look. 'And any marauding GIs as well!'

Limey stared back at him cheekily.

'Alright, you guys, you can fall out. And remember – no dames. We move out at dawn!'

'Well, skipper, what do you think?' van Fleet took a last spoonful of hash from the can and tossed it into the trash container already filled to the top with similar cans, T-Force's supper.

'Jesus, Clarry,' Hardt replied, his face still flushed from having had to deal with the giggling, simpering women. He took his boots from the scrubbed wooden kitchen table and swallowed the last of his ration chocolate bar. 'I don't know whether I'm coming or going. We get hit this afternoon by a lot of kids in short pants. We lose our guide so that I don't know where the hell those Hungarians are. And now *that!*' He indicated the giggling and cooing from upstairs. 'The love call of a sick cow!'

'It's nature, skipper,' van Fleet said, obviously amused at the Major's embarrassment.

'It goddamwell might be! But with half the guys so horny since Germany that they can't think of anything else but tail, it doesn't make for a very taut ship, Clarry.'

Van Fleet smiled. 'What's the drill, then, skipper?'

'We play it cool. We'll take it in turns to check the sentries throughout the night, and hope that we can make it till dawn without those Russian cowboys, the Cossacks hitting us. And you'd better pray, Clarry, that when the morning comes that those dames upstairs haven't put an end to T-Force,' he added grimly.

Van Fleet, trying to keep a straight face as the first of the beds upstairs started to creak significantly, asked innocently, 'How do you mean, skipper?'

'In bed, Clarry. That's what I mean – *in bed!*...'

DAY THREE

'Look George, you know you are your own worse enemy. But I won't go into that now. All I'll say is this. From here on – I'm not going to tolerate one more fool action like this from you. Make a horse's ass out of yourself again and you're *out!*'

Gen. Eisenhower to Gen. Patton,
May 8th, 1945.

ONE

Somewhere in the darkened old house, bed-springs were creaking crazily like red hot pistons.

'Cor,' Limey whispered, 'get a load of that! Old Wheels must be going at it like a ruddy fiddler's elbow.'

'Was … was sagst du, Sasser?' the nubile little blonde asked, as they lay side by side in the rumpled bed, naked and damp with sweat, smoking their cigarettes and watching the glowing ends in the darkness in pleasurable contentment.

'I said like a fiddler's elbow.' Limey puffed hard at his cigarette so that she could see the crude gesture he made in the red glow. 'Like that.'

She giggled softly. *'Ja, ja, ich verstehe.'*

'Versteh – plenty jig-jig?'

'Wir machten auch viel jig-jig,' she said.

'Yer, and we're gonna make a lot more in a mo, baby, as soon as I've put out this fag,' Limey growled and putting out one hand squeezed her right nipple experimentally.

The girl gasped pleasurably. With a squeak of the ancient bedsprings she turned towards him and ran a damp, hot hand across his chest, then began to let it run slowly lower.

'Cheeky little sexpot,' Limey said. He gave a mock sigh. 'The things I do for England.' Already he started to feel the first vague stirrings of new desire. He stubbed out his cigarette half smoked. 'Who needs fags anyway?' he said to no one in particular and turned towards her expectant body. 'The other's better any day of the week.'

But that dawn Limey was not fated to get any more of the 'other'. Just as he began to stroke her swollen breasts, he heard the whinny of a horse outside. The sound was startlingly clear and unexpected at that time.

At his side, the girl's body went tense. He could feel her heart begin to beat at a tremendous rate. *'Die Kusacken!'* she whispered fearfully.

'Eh?'

'Die Kusacken.' She pushed him away and sat up in bed, her hands covering her breasts fearfully, her eyes wide and staring in the moonlight which came through the little barred window. *'Die Kusacken sind draussen!'*

'Cossacks!' Limey sat up suddenly too. 'I'll

be stuffed. What sodding next. Some folk have no consideration.' Hastily, while the girl cowered behind him, Limey padded to the window in his bare feet and peered out.

Nothing. The countryside, bathed in the silver light of the waning moon, was empty. Nothing stirred. Limey rubbed his eyes. 'Am I dreaming? I'm bloody well sure, I heard a nag out there.'

Then he spotted the man, his gaze attracted by a suddenly gleam of silver – perhaps a knife. He was crouched in a pool of darkness cast by some sort of an outhouse, some fifty yards from the house. And there was another man, kneeling just behind him. 'Oh, sweet Jesus,' he cursed.

Hurriedly he swung round and held his fingers to his lips to indicate to the girl she shouldn't call out. 'Not a ruddy sound,' he whispered, 'or the buggers'll rush us before we have a chance. *Versteh – nix sagen!*'

She nodded her understanding. '*Ja, ja, ich verstehe. Aber ich komme mit,*' she added urgently as Limey started to scramble feverishly into his clothes. Naked as she was, she sprang out of bed and joined him as he stumbled to the door, fumbling for his hand.

'Oh sodding hell,' Limey cursed, 'heaven help a sailor on a night like this. The CO'll have me by the goolies for this caper.'

But Major Hardt was too concerned by Limey's news to be worried about the naked, shivering blonde standing next to him as he reported what he had seen in the garden outside. 'You *are* sure, Limey?' he snapped swiftly, when Limey was finished.

'Of course, I'm sure, sir. There's somebody out there, and there are others by the half-tracks.'

'Balls!'

'And they must be the Cossacks. I heard an old nag whinnying out there too. She thinks they are anyway.' He indicated the ashen-faced girl.

'For Chrissake, throw that blanket over her, will you! How can I think looking at all that meat.'

'Do you think they've got us, sir?' Limey asked anxiously, doing as he was ordered.

'I don't know. Van Fleet, have a look-see. But don't show yourself, I don't want them rushing us before we can get organised. Jesus, I could kick myself for not having dismounted the fifty calibres before we bedded down for the night. Now all we've got is our personal weapons.'

A few moments later van Fleet returned. His face was grim and Hardt did not even have to ask him whether the house were surrounded or not. 'The back too – did you check the back?' he asked urgently.

Van Fleet nodded glumly. 'Yeah, skipper, they're there too – in force.'

'Oh brother, this is a real snafu.' Hardt pulled himself together. In the silence outside he could hear them moving ever closer to the house. He had to act soon. 'Limey,' he ordered, 'upstairs at the double and get the rest of the guys out of the sack toot sweet!'

Limey was off like a shot. 'Clarry, rouse Big Red, I want him down here with the crew of Old Baldy. Your guys can take the upper floor. But for Chrissake, don't alert the Cossacks before we're in position or there'll be hell to pay.'

'Wilco, skipper.'

Van Fleet disappeared too. Hardt turned to the trembling girl. 'Under that table – *quick!*' he commanded.

She might not have understood the words, but she understood the gesture well enough. She scrambled under the broad kitchen table hastily and carelessly. Hardt could see that she was a true blonde. But he had no time for such things now. He grabbed his grease gun, clicked off the safety and turning off the light, ran, crouched low, towards the window. Carefully he undid the catches and opened it a little. What he saw made him gasp. The silver gardens seemed full of stealthily moving men. There were scores of them. The numbers of his T-Force were pathetic in comparison.

Hardly daring to breathe, he opened the window and poked the muzzle of his grease gun through the open space with great care. Above him he could hear the men getting out of bed, their own and the women's cursing, softly and fumbling for their weapons. It was a rude awakening after a night of love, he told himself. But if they didn't get a move on, they wouldn't see another such night.

And then it happened. On the second floor a woman screamed, loud, high and hysterical, as she saw the Russians coming through the garden. In an instant, the hysterical screaming was taken up by the other women, panicked by the thought of what was going to happen to them in a few minutes.

'Balls, that's torn it,' Hardt cried and squeezed the trigger of his grease gun as the Russians rushed forward. The first row of Cossacks went down abruptly, as if they had been scythed, arms and legs flailing in sudden frenetic confusion. But behind them the others came, running now, stumbling over the bodies of their comrades writhing in agony on the grass; but coming on all the same.

The burst of fire was all the command the rest of T-Force needed. In rapid succession the veterans each smashed down a window in a sudden crash of glass and opened fire. More and more of the Cossacks went down, skidding to a sudden stop, yelping with agony or falling flat on their faces without a sound. But with the reckless courage of their kind, they kept on coming, yelling furiously, swinging their great curved sabres, seized by the atavistic fury of their wild frontier forefathers.

Just before dawn they broke through the front door, around which were littered their dead and dying. A screaming Cossack on a great white stallion scrambled up the steps, his body clasped close to the horse's right side. Big Red didn't hesitate. He let the horse have a burst in the face. It reared high on its hind legs, whinnying with unbearable pain, the blood spouting from the multiple wounds in its face. The Cossack dropped from the mortally wounded horse and tried to scramble for safety. Too late! Three quarters of a ton of horse crashed upon him. He screamed piteously – once – and lay still, crushed to death.

Another Cossack tried it. As his horse mounted the steps, he vaulted over its head like a circus performer and came running at the retreating T-Force men, lashing his great knout from side to side, its lead-tipped leather thongs hissing frighteningly through the air. A T-Force man screamed and went reeling back, his face streaming with blood, as if he had been clawed by a lion. The Cossack's dark face gleamed with triumph. But not for long. Triggerman let him have a burst in the belly. 'Now take that, you Russian bastard!' he snarled.

The Russian staggered forward, hands clasping his ruined belly. Suddenly his knees buckled beneath him like those of a new-born foal. His hands sank wearily from his stomach and his intestines spilled onto the floor in front of him like an evil, pulsating blue-grey snake. Next moment he fell flat on his face, tripped up by his own guts, and lay there panting shallowly, until Hardt put a bullet through his head at twenty yards' range.

But despite their terrible casualties, the Cossacks kept on attacking like gamblers who knew they could not win, but who were prepared to throw away their last penny because the realised that life held nothing more for them but this. Yard by yard they pressed the T-Force men up into the second floor, where the women, half naked for the most part, were treating the casualties as best they could.

Grimly Hardt fought back, knowing that once the Cossacks had pinned them down upstairs, they could do what they wanted. It would only take one of them to find the incendiary grenades stowed away in the back of Old Baldy and to realise what they were for. The whole damned place would be on fire in a matter of minutes! Then they would be forced either to come down or die the most terrible of death. As the little Englishman, fighting at his side, gasped, 'Jesus, sir, if this is peacetime, give me the ruddy big war any sodding day – it's bloody safer.'

'You can say that again, Limey!' Hardt replied through gritted teeth and fired another burst at the Russians swarming up the stairs.

By dawn the handful of T-Force men and the frightened sobbing women were pinned down in two rooms on the second floor at the back of the house. Up the passage the Cossacks had set up a heavy machine gun –

probably a spandau, Hardt guessed from the rapid high-pitched snarl – and were systematically blasting the walls apart. Overhead, the shaken defenders could hear the Cossacks removing the roof tiles prior to making an attempt to break in through the ceiling. Hardt realised that it was only a matter of time now before they would have to surrender or die where they were – and he had the women to think of too. Already several of them had been wounded and lay gasping on the debris-littered floor while their friends, crouched low in the dust-filled air, attempted to bandage them up the best they could.

'What do you think our chances are, skipper?' van Fleet asked, his face covered like a clown's in a thick layer of white dust.

'Dicey,' Hardt answered, fitting his last magazine. 'Five minutes more is my guess and then the bastards'll rush us.' He raised his voice above the terrific racket of the heavy machine gun. 'Red.'

'Sir?' the big NCO answered, wiping the blood away from the cut on his forehead.

'You and Trigger get yourselves into the centre of the floor. Don't expose yourself unnecessary, but once they try to come through the ceiling,' he pointed upwards to where the sound of the Russian infiltrators were getting louder, 'give the buggers all you've got.'

'Right, sir,' Red answered promptly. 'Come on, Trigger. Now you can really show how good you are with that popgun of yours.'

Trigger made an obscene gesture.

Big Red grinned wearily. 'And your mother too, Trigger,' he replied easily.

Hardt shook his head. 'Jesus, Clarry, aren't they a great bunch of guys. The second day of peace and they're in the middle of all this shit, yet you'd think it was only a goddam training exercise!'

'Yessir.'

'Okay, the rest of you,' Hardt bellowed, 'save your ammo now. We haven't much left and we'll need all we've got in a minute.'

Instinctively the women tensed like the handful of weary defenders. It was now or never. But nothing happened!

Gross and ponderous as he was, the Fat One had been the first to realise what was happening as the two ancient wood-burning trucks, commandeered from the German farmers, approached the crossroads. 'It's them!' he had cried.

'Who?' Dieter, sitting next to him in the big cab next to the driver, Wiebke, had asked.

'The *Amis*, you asparagus Tarzan – they're in that house out there,' he had indicated the lonely house to their right from which the scarlet stab and flash of small arms fire was coming. 'And they're in trouble!'

'It's Vlasov's Cossacks,' Wiebke had yelled, slowing down instinctively. 'Those horses over there in the glade – they're theirs.'

'Those renegades,' the Fat One had snarled. 'I'll teach those slave pigs. All right, you silly cow, don't just sit there – take the truck off the road.'

'Where to?' Wiebke had asked.

'Across the field to where those half-tracks of theirs are parked. *And move it!*'

Now they were in position to the attackers' rear. Hastily the Fat One disposed his force in a semi-circle around the half-tracks. With a grunt he clambered up into the first one, commanding Dieter to take over the 50 calibre machine gun in the second vehicle. Expertly he unlocked the heavy machine gun, for like all the Werewolves he'd been trained to use most known enemy weapons. Down below a curly-haired boy prepared to fire his *panzerfaust*. 'All right,' he cried. *'NOW!'*

The youth with the *panzerfaust* placed it on his shoulder and fired. A jet of bright flame shot from the bazooka. The awkward bomb hurtled across the field, trailing angry red sparks after it. With a thick crump it exploded in the crowded doorway. Cossacks reeled back on all sides. In the next instant, the rest of the *Kommando* opened fire. The unexpected volley caught the attackers completely by surprise. Abruptly everything was panic-stricken confusion.

The Fat One, the sweat streaming down his face in thick rivulets, swung the 50 calibre from side to side like a crazy man, spraying the Russians on the roof with lead. They flew in every direction, screaming as they were carried over the side, as if they were flies swatted away by some gigantic hand.

Abruptly the Cossacks broke. They came streaming out of the house, dropping their loot in their fear, clawing and tearing at each other, trying frantically to get out of that murderous fire. The Fat One let them have another burst, then he dropped the smoking machine gun and bellowed. 'Enough, enough... Cease firing!... You Wiebke and Trudi, off to those horses and release them... Chase them away!'

The two girls ran off to carry out his orders, while the Fat One watched the beaten Cossacks streaming into the fields to the far side of the house, cut off from their mounts by the new enemy who had attacked them so surprisingly from the rear. Finally, satisfied that they would present no further danger this day, he called: 'All right, they look okay in that house – we've saved the *Amis'* skins, I think.' He grinned suddenly but there was nothing very pleasant about his grin. 'We've got to look after our new allies, haven't we?'

The others laughed softly.

'Schoen!' he snapped. 'Back to the trucks. Let's get out of here before they see us. We mustn't make it too obvious, must we?'

Five minutes later *Werewolf Kommando Funf* had disappeared into the new, bright morning, as abruptly as they had appeared.

'Well, what in hell's name do you make of that, Clarry?' Hardt asked in complete bewilderment, as he and van Fleet, grease guns at the ready, made their way cautiously down the bullet-pocked corridor, heavy with the stink of cordite, and littered with dead Russians. Behind them there was no sound save the bitter sobs of a dying woman calling over and over again for a *'Mama'*, who would never come now.

'God only knows, skipper,' van Fleet answered, as puzzled as his CO. 'One minute the buggers were there, holding us by the short and curlies, the next they were bugging out like a bat out of hell!'

'Yeah.' Hardt lowered his grease gun and breathed out hard. The house was empty of Cossacks. He pushed his helmet back from his scarred, bald head. 'One thing is for sure, Clarry.'

'What's that, skipper?'

Hardt peered into the flat dusty rays of the first sun, squinting a little, as if he hoped to see something out there which would explain everything. 'Whoever attacked the Russians from the rear was Kraut. I heard German distinctly.' He swung round and faced the younger officer. 'Now what do you make of that, Clarry?'

But van Fleet's sole reaction was a puzzled shake of his handsome head.

TWO

The little single-engined L-5 spotted them two hours later. The plane came in low from the west, waggled its wings once and then at almost stalling speed hovered over the two half-tracks so that the T-Force men manning the machine guns could see the stars which identified it as belonging to the Army Air Corps. 'One of ours, sir,' Big Red yelled excitedly and Triggerman relaxed his pressure on the trigger of the 50 calibre.

'Wheels, pull over, willya,' Hardt ordered.

The little driver reacted at once. The two vehicles came to a stop at the side of the dusty road, while the L-5 wheeled to the east and came in again, its signal lamp flickering.

'Read it, Limey!' Hardt commanded hastily.

Standing upright in the half-track, his eyes screwed up against the bright sunlight, Limey read off the Morse letter 'E-U-R-E-K-A.' As the plane flashed overhead, he shouted above the roar of its motor. 'He wants us to use the Eureka, sir, I think.'

'Okay, Limey, get on the stick,' Hardt cried as the little artillery spotter plane sailed high into the sky, 'break out the Eureka.'

The Eureka device had been developed by the British in forty-three for instant communication between secret agents on the ground and controller in the air. It had obviated the risky, long-winded business of communicating with base by means of shortwave radio. In forty-four American

OSS agents behind the German lines had used it successfully up to a height of thirty thousand feet in Belgium and Northern France. Patton, always eager to try out new devices, had obtained one for T-Force and Hardt had employed it in the last stages of the campaign in Southern Germany to communicate instantly with the General, who had not shunned the danger of flying deep into enemy territory in order to obtain the valuable information that his long-range penetration group could provide.

Now, with Hardt crouching at his side, Limey put the top-secret device into operation and listened for the pilot's first booming words. They weren't very encouraging.

'Hello T-Force. This is Charley One. The General wants you to know that your Red friends are on to you. *Over!*'

'Clarify, *over,*' Limey barked.

'Source Pilsen has informed Red friends of your mission. *Over.*'

'Bollocks,' Limey cursed and told Hardt what the pilot had said.

'Ask him what our Red friends intend to do, Limey?' Hardt said urgently.

'Eliminate them first,' the pilot answered easily. 'The Honkys are for the chop ... then it's the General's guess you might get lucky that way too.' He chuckled metallically. 'Nice way to spend VE Day Three, ain't it? *Over.*'

Limey muttered an obscenity and relayed the pilot's words to a worried Hardt.

'Smart guy,' Hardt said. 'Okay, ask him if he has any idea of the Honky's position. Tell him we've lost our guide.'

Limey spoke into the apparatus hastily and, flicking the switch, waited for the pilot's answer.

It was disappointing. 'No savvy, Major. The General has been giving his radio interception team hell this morning trying to get a radio fix on the Honkys. But they must be on radio silence or something. It was no deal.'

Hardt absorbed the information quickly, while the little monoplane flew round in a slow circle and came in again. 'All right then,' he transmitted through Limey, 'can you do me a favour? *Over.*'

'Sure,' the pilot answered with the easy carelessness of his kind. 'Nothing's too good for the boys in the service. What do you want, Major?'

Hastily Hardt explained that he wanted a forward recon of the Hungarian positions. The L-5 could cover the ground it would take his half-tracks half a day to cover in less than an hour.

'Sure,' the pilot answered. 'I guess it's against orders. But hellfire, what are orders for, if not to be broken. Okay, Major, this is the deal. I've got gas for ninety minutes. That gives me about sixty minutes' flying time over this area before I'll have to head back to base. You can expect me to contact you again by zero ten hundred. Kay?'

Hardt signalled his agreement.

'Kay, then wish me luck. *Over and out.*'

One last time the L-5 came in low. Hardt caught a glimpse of a white grinning face behind the gleaming perspex of the cockpit and then with a cheeky final wiggle of his wings, the pilot took her high into the bright blue morning sky. Minutes later he had disappeared to the east and the little convoy began to move cautiously down the highway once more.

Al Higgs had been an artillery spotter since the Battle of the Bulge and he had a silver plate in the back of his crew-cut head to remind him of his start in that highly dangerous, short-lived profession. But in spite of his easy casual manner, he was a very professional pilot, who had survived the murderous Rhineland campaign and the one into Central Europe, which had followed, because of his attention to detail: the unusually shaped bush in the corner of a field, which was a quadruple Kraut flak cannon; the groups of dark figures below standing in pairs, what looked like long bars across their shoulders – spandau teams waiting for unwary pilots to come in low and check them out so that they could blast them out of the air; the hard white trail high in the sky above him – a fighter plane trying to get into position so that it could come hurtling out of the sun, machine guns chattering.

Al Higgs knew all the tricks – that was why he had survived five months of combat. Now, although this was the third day of peace and the *Luftwaffe* was finished, he set about the task of finding the Third Hungarian Army as if he were operating under wartime conditions. Flying very low, following the contours of the hills exactly, never following the whole length of a road (the way to make a spotter plane an obvious target for any flak gunner), but zig-zagging across it at erratic intervals, one eye on the ground and one on his rear mirror in case a Messerschmitt might appear, he set about his task.

The minutes passed rapidly. Now the little plane was cruising some thirty miles west of Prague. Far to the east, Higgs could just make out the smoke haze of what might well have been the capital's industrial suburbs. But then his attention was distracted by the first obvious signs of a large number of men – the characteristic deep-pressed trails in the fields on both sides of the road to Prague. He came down lower. His quick eyes spotted the little horse-drawn carts in the cover of the nearest hedge. He gunned his engine like a hunter might strike a tree loudly to scare out a rabbit. A handful of soldiers burst out of a clump of dusty firs and stared up at him. He throttled back and let them have a good look at the white stars underneath his wings. The men dropped their already raised rifles and began waving their arms frantically, big grins on their faces as they stared upwards.

He did a tight loop and came in again, even lower this time. More and more soldiers came out of the firs and he could see the camouflaged howitzers deeper in the wood. He'd found the Third Hungarian Army at last!

Suddenly the cheering men below began to scatter. Dropping their rifles they dived back into the firs. A man, slower than the rest, gesticulated towards the sky and then he disappeared after his comrades. Al Higgs flashed a glance into his rear mirror and gasped with shock. Above him the sky was filled with the black shapes of bombers, grouped in attack formation, while little fat-bellied fighters wheeled in and out of the formations like terriers ensuring that their charges did not straggle.

'Holy cow!' Al Higgs cried and swung his plane round, 'what the hell is the Red Air Force doing here?'

His answer came a moment later. Abruptly the first formation of Stormovik dive-bombers seemed to fall out of the sky. Sirens howling, they descended upon the Hungarian positions like predatory black hawks, engines going flat out. Just when it seemed as if the formation leader would go plummeting into the ground at four hundred mph, the pilot levelled out. For one fleeting moment, the Stormovik hovered there. A myriad deadly black eggs tumbled from its camouflaged belly. And then the plane was soaring high into the bright-blue of the sky while the world below was suddenly transformed into a crazy, heaving, murderous chaos.

'Jesus H. Christ!' Al Higgs breathed as dive-bomber after dive-bomber pounded the Hungarian positions. 'The poor bastards – they haven't got a chance!'

But as the heavy bombers followed, intent

on carrying out *Stavka's* orders that the pathetic little Third Hungarian Army should be wiped out before the Americans could contact it, a Yak fighter spotted Higgs's plane. It dived immediately to discover who this observer of the massacre was.

Al Higgs's ears were shocked by the sharp implosive boom, like the sound of an express entering a tunnel. He flashed a look upwards, his face darkened by the enormous rushing shadow. Instinctively he let the L-5 fall as the Yak's slip-stream caught him.

For a second the Czech horizon oscillated while Higgs fought the steering column with all his strength, trying to prevent the L-5 from hitting the deck. He had just controlled the plane when the Yak came barrelling in again, the four machine guns mounted in its wings, spitting violet fire. 'The crazy bastard – he's gonna shoot me down,' Al Higgs yelled, speaking to himself in the fashion of all pilots.

Convulsively he tightened his grip on the column. Sweat trickled down the small of his back as he brought the L-5 down to fifty feet, the usual defensive manoeuvre against an attacking fighter. Below the green fields rolled away at dizzying speed. Higgs had no eyes for them; only the black speck in his rear mirror, growing large by the instant.

This time the Yak came in slower, its undercarriage down so that it wouldn't overshoot the much slower L-5. Higgs threw a quick glance at his altimeter. The needle shuddered at seventy-five feet. Dare he take her down any further? He made a decision. Behind him the Yak's wings crackled with angry lights. Red tracer cut the air like a swarm of furious hornets. Higgs made several swift movements. The little engine almost cut out. Like a stone the L-5 dropped. Higgs stomach flew up to his throat, or so it seemed. Below him the ground thrust upwards terrifyingly. Next instant the fat-bellied Yak, its guns still chattering furiously, shot above him. The L-5 trembled furiously. Just in time, Higgs gave her full throttle. He was pinned back against his seat as the engine regained its fully thrust. Steeply the tough little spotter plane rose up into the air once again.

But the Yak pilot did not react so swiftly. He was not used to tackling experts like Higgs. In the last moment he saw his danger. But it was too late. His undercarriage caught the tops of a group of firs. In a flash it was ripped off like cardboard. The Yak turned over on its belly. Desperately the pilot fought the controls. But the fighter did not respond. A white stream of glycol shot out of its damaged radial engine. It covered the cockpit in a white layer. Blinded, the pilot plunged to the earth. The plane smashed into the ground. Slithering crazily from side the side, the stricken Yak tore forward, trailing a huge cloud of dust behind it. With a wild, rending crash it rammed into a thick oak. Next instant it was a seething mass of angry flames.

'Stupid bastard–' the words died on Higgs' lips, as the burst of vicious fire from the Yak's wingman ripped the wooden flame of the L-5 apart. His spine arched in a taut bow. Thick blood spurted from the side of his mouth, as his head fell to one side. Crazily the L-5 plunged from the sky, bearing with it the first American air casualty of a new war...

THREE

'Well skipper,' van Fleet demanded. 'What gives?'

Hardt lowered his binoculars. Ahead of the parked half-tracks, the Czech plain sweltered in the midday heat; the sun cut the eyes like the blade of a sharp knife. He blinked. His eyelids closed and opened several times. 'Nothing gives,' he answered a little bitterly. 'Not a sign of him and it's two hours since he first contacted us. According to what he said, he would be out of gas now, if–'

'He were still coming back,' van Fleet completed the sentence for him.

'Yep,' Hardt rapped, suddenly a little angry for some reason he could not explain to himself. 'So we can conclude, can't we, that he isn't coming back.' He shrugged. 'Why, I wouldn't know.'

'Perhaps an accident. Or perhaps he simply had to abort the mission,' van Fleet said hastily, trying to cheer the Major up.

'I don't know, Clarry, I just don't know. All I know is that this darned mission has been jinxed right from the goddam start. The poor jerk has run into trouble, I can feel it in my bones.' He slumped back against the hot metal of the half-track. All around him, the T-Force men, sweating in the midday heat, were eating cold hash in a heavy silence, while Big Red checked the dressings of the wounded. For what seemed a long time there was no sound save the chatter of birds in the trees above them and the clatter of the men's spoons in the hash cans.

'What now, skipper?' van Fleet asked the question which Hardt had been expecting for the last hour now.

Hardt lit a *Camel* slowly and carefully, as if the operation required some attention. 'We're making lousy time. My guess is that we've only got about twenty hours left. We could go back, but I guess Old Blood and Guts wouldn't like that too much. And as a Regular I've got to consider my 201 File, haven't I?' He grinned wearily.

Van Fleet grinned back at him.

'And hell, I hate to go back empty-handed, Clarry. Still I've got to think of the men. Apart from Big Red, none of them are Regulars. Why should they risk their necks anymore, Clarry? This is peacetime after all, dammit all!'

'Why don't you ask them, skipper?' van Fleet suggested softly.

Hardt tugged his nose thoughtfully for a moment, then he rose to his feet. 'Fellers, listen to me for a minute.'

The T-Force men looked up at him, spoons still clutched in their hands.

'I'll be honest with you. I don't think that flyboy is coming back,' Hardt explained. 'So that means I don't know where the Hungarians are. I don't even know whether the Russians have reached them yet. But they might well have. So we might be trying to contact them for nothing.' He stared around at their tired, sweat-lathered faces. 'All the same I'd like to go on. T-Force never failed on a mission in wartime. I'd hate to start the peace on a wrong foot.' He laughed a little wearily. 'Still I don't want to risk your lives again like last night. But if you were prepared to go on with me for another – say – twenty hours, I'd be very pleased. If we didn't find the Hungarians by then, that would be it. We'd turn for home toot sweet.' He paused expectantly.

'T-Force has never aborted a mission yet, sir!' Big Red announced suddenly, straightening up to his full height, clenching his hamlike fist threateningly. 'Speaking for the rest of the fellers, I can say we're with you. Aren't we, youse guys?' he growled, his voice full of heavy menace.

'Soddit, Sarge,' Limey quipped, 'but you're such an awful convincing speaker, you are!'

The ice was broken. Laughing and joking with one another, the weary veterans set about preparing to move on, spurred on by the CO's final promise that they would 'find the Honkys this day!'...

But Major Hardt would not have been so confident if at that same moment he had been able to listen to the conversation taking place between the Commander of the Ukrainian Front and Colonel Rurik of the 1st Guards Cavalry Regiment in a little shell-shattered Czech farmhouse some ten miles east of Prague. In the distance a German 88mm was pounding away at regular intervals, manned by some of Field Marshal Schoerner's fanatical rearguard, who had still refused to surrender to the advancing Russians.

But the bemedalled, barrel-chested Commander of the Ukrainian Front had no ears for the guns, nor eyes for the long columns of dusty infantry in earth-coloured blouses, slouching by on their way to Prague, drinking their daily ration of vodka straight from the bottle, munching sunflower seed and spitting at regular intervals in the Russian fashion. His attention was concentrated solely on Colonel Rurik.

Rurik was worth looking at. Taller than the average Russian, he was handsome with bold black eyes and dark curly hair. His good looks had broken down the resistance of many a pretty woman and his chest revealed that he was as bold on the battlefield as he was in bed. It was covered with decorations, gained on every European front since he had entered the battle for Mother Russia as a twenty-four-year-old tank captain in 1941.

Since Stalingrad he had served with the Ukrainian Front and the Army Commander knew him as one of his bravest and boldest officers, the idol of his men for his courage on the battlefield. In February 1945 Rurik had been given command of the élite Guards Cavalry Regiment after he had repelled an all-out attack by the Tigers of the Adolf Hitler Bodyguard in Hungary, sending the Germans' best SS troops fleeing back for their lives, completely broken. The action had gained him his third Hero of the Soviet Union and the Army Commander's considered opinion that Rurik would be a general himself by the time he was in his mid-thirties.

'I have called you,' the Army Commander said after they had exchanged the usual small talk, 'because I have an important mission for your Guards.'

Rurik's eyes flashed. 'Prague, Comrade Army Commander?'

'No, Rurik. Further!'

'Further.' Rurik grinned, flashing his

excellent white teeth. 'New York perhaps, Comrade Army Commander?' He laughed easily with the confidence of a man who had never failed, either in bed or on the battlefield.

'Not just yet, my dear Rurik. Perhaps one day soon but for the time being we will be a little more modest in our objectives.'

Outside some bandy-legged Siberians were lining up a handful of blond boys in dusty, ragged field-grey against the wall of the shattered farmhouse. The Army Commander did not even notice; such things were a daily occurrence in his Army. Instead he walked across to the map spread out on the kitchen table, held in place by a crucifix torn from the wall and an old flat-iron. He stabbed a nicotine-brown forefinger at it. 'One hour ago,' he announced, 'the First Air Fleet attacked the Third Hungarian Army here. They had attempted to make contact with the Americans so that they could surrender to them. One hour ago we taught them that Comrade Stalin' – he said the name as if it were in italics – 'does not like dirty little games of that kind.'

'Agreed, Comrade Army Commander,' Rurik answered stiffly, his respect for the Soviet leader clearly visible in his suddenly hard eyes.

'According to our latest aerial reconnaissance of their position, there isn't much left of them. The survivors are straggling through the countryside everywhere. They have abandoned whatever heavy equipment survived our attack. However,' he raised his brown forefinger warningly, 'some of their staff have important information – a paper – which must not fall into unauthorized hands. I can't tell you much, but you will receive instructions on what to look for?'

'You mean this is connected with my mission, Comrade Army Commander?'

Outside the Siberians had formed a rough line, in front of the pale young Germans, their gleaming faces completely impassive.

'Yes, this is to be your mission. You will find the paper and bring it back to this headquarters immediately. You will take half a battalion of your Joseph Stalin tanks and half a battalion of motorized Guards infantry. I think that should be sufficient to deal with whatever Fritzes you might bump into on your way.'

'The Fritzes!' Rurik puffed out his lips contemptuously. 'The Fritzes I can deal with, with one hand tied behind my back, Comrade.'

The Army Commander smiled, pleased with his choice of leader for the mission. Rurik wouldn't let him down. He'd better not. Stalin was already breathing down his neck about the Molotov Paper and even a successful Army Commander, who had had nothing but victories for the last two years, knew better than to offend the undersized pock-marked Georgian whom they all called 'leather-face' (behind his back – and very softly).

Outside one of the German POWs, who didn't look a day older than fifteen, was on his knees in the white dust, hands clasped together in the classic pose of supplication, tears streaming down his ashen face. The Siberians watched him stony-faced.

'Good, good,' the Army Commander said. 'Swing round the western suburbs of the capital. I don't want you to get bogged down in Prague. The situation there is reported to be confused. You know what idiots these Czechs are.' He spat contemptuously on the kitchen floor. 'Take the road to Pilsen – the main highway, here. Now, we have no exact information where the Hungarians' HQ was located. But you can guess how you'll find whatever staff survived of that comic operetta army?'

'Naturally, Comrade Army Commander. Just like at Stalingrad, they will seize the motor transport and take off, leaving the rank and file to look after themselves the best they can.'

'Correct.'

'Be on the look-out for motor transport. Without doubt it will contain the people you will be looking for – the staff of the Third Hungarian Army.' He took a sealed envelope from his breast pocket and handed it to Rurik. 'In that you will find a description of the Paper you are looking for!'

'*Spasiva.*' Rurik answered smartly and noted – with a hardly contained gasp of surprise – the seal of the Kremlin, before he tucked it away carefully in his pocket.

'One thing, Rurik,' the Army Commander said warningly. 'We have information from a source at the American Army HQ at Pilsen that they too have sent a small armoured force to contact the Hungarians. We have no idea where they are and neither have the Americans, although they tried to communicate with their men by air this morning.' He chuckled. It wasn't a pleasant sound. 'Unfortunately their pilot met with a little accident. However you can take it the Americans are still out there somewhere, looking for the Hungarians.'

'And if I bump into them with my Guards, Comrade Army Commander?' Rurik asked smartly.

Outside the Siberian officer rapped out a brisk order. There was the rattle of rifle fire. The German POWs against the wall were galvanised into sudden frantic action, like puppets in the hands of a crazy puppeteer. The Army Commander waited until the noise had died away, then he said baldly: 'You will kill them, Rurik...'

FOUR

'The Hungarians,' Hardt announced numbly, as the first half-track rumbled through the lunar landscape, pitted with fresh-brown holes like the work of some monstrous mole. The savagely mutilated dead were sprawled carelessly everywhere.

The raid had caught them completely by surprise. They had been slaughtered in their holes like animals, like cattle in an abattoir, the pits half-filled with the viscous red gore. Others had tried to make a break for it. They hadn't got far. The pathetic bundles of bodies lay along the road, next to the corpses of skinny-ribbed horses and buckled bicycles. Time and time again Wheels, sweating and cursing, had to swing his wheel from one side to the other to avoid the bodies, while the T-Force men held on and observed in silent horror with wide, staring eyes.

They passed a howitzer battery caught out in the open, a hopelessly confused mess of metal and man welded together in death, one solitary human hand, fingers extended, reaching out to the heavens as if in that moment of sudden death its owner had begged for mercy. But there had been no mercy. The harsh burning sky looked down upon the manner of their death without remorse.

In heavy silence the little convoy rolled down the endless white road, through the piled dead of the Third Hungarian Army, looking for a sign of life which would indicate that there was still some purpose to their mission. But it seemed hopeless. The Czech countryside was empty of the living. It had, it appeared, become one great gruesome graveyard.

'Well, what do you think, Clarry?' Major Hardt broke the silence at last, his voice hushed in the presence of so much death. 'Do you think there's a chance that any of them survived?'

Van Fleet licked his dry lips, his face very pale. 'I don't think so, skipper. Whoever did it–'

'The Russians,' Hardt interrupted tonelessly.

'Well, then the Russians did a good job. It's worse than the Falaise Pocket slaughter in Normandy back in forty-four.' He paused momentarily and stared at a headless body, still propped upright somehow or other at the side of the road. 'I hardly think anybody could have survived this, skipper. I'm afraid we've had it.'

But five minutes later, just as they began to enter a shattered smoking hamlet, Lieutenant van Fleet was proved wrong. They had started to clatter along a cobbled road, strewn with blown-down signal wires, when there was an abrupt shout. Hardt and van Fleet swung their heads round in unison.

A man was staggering towards them out of a side alley, his arms stretched out so that he did not lose his balance, his high riding boots making a deliberate, shuffling clatter on the cobbles, as if he could only move forward step by step by a sheer effort of will.

'Hold it, Wheels!' Hardt yelled.

The little ex-cabbie hit the brakes. The half-track jerked to a stop as Hardt and van Fleet dropped over the side, grease guns at the ready.

But they dropped them almost immediately. They knew instinctively the man staggering towards them was dying, his legs moving with the lunatic deliberation of a slow-motion movie, the dark blood streaming from his head and shoulders, leaving a wavering trail behind him on the road.

'Hardt, grab him!' van Fleet yelled urgently.

Hardt dived forward and caught the man before he fell. Carefully he lowered him to the ground and looked down at his dark face. The right eye was a pink pulsating pit, filled with a nauseating mixture of blood and white bone splinters. 'Give me your helmet, Clarry,' Hardt commented.

Hastily van Fleet removed the helmet and lifting the dying man's head, Hardt slipped it carefully under.

The man's other eye flicked open. He mumbled something in a language the two officers could not understand; then he licked his scummed, split lips and said weakly:

'Thank you, I knew you would come.'

'You speak English?' van Fleet asked stupidly.

'I did a post-graduate year at USC,' the Hungarian answered. 'A long time ago.' He tried to smile, but failed lamentably.

'Take it easy. Don't talk,' Hardt commanded. He unscrewed his canteen and lifting the man's head pressed it to his lips. The Hungarian drank greedily and clumsily, the water spilling down the front of his bloody tunic.

'Clarry, double back to the half-track. Get the sulphur, bandages and the hypo. I'll give him a shot–'

'No,' the Hungarian tore his lips away from the canteen like a greedy baby forcing itself to relinquish the nipple. 'No, no use. There is no time for that.'

'But–'

'I beg you ... I haven't much time left. Listen, Americans. We knew you would come.'

'We?' Hardt asked.

'Yes, the staff of the Third Army. I was General Jerzy's adjutant.'

Hardt flashed van Fleet a swift look; they had found the people they were looking for.

'But when you didn't come that first day, we started to worry–' his body was suddenly racked by a bout of coughing. A trickle of pinkish froth came out of the side of his mouth. The Hungarian had obviously been wounded in the lung too. 'We decided,' he gasped, recovering himself a little, 'to get rid of the Crown and the Paper–'

'The Paper?' van Fleet interrupted.

The Hungarian ignored the question, as if he knew he had very little time left and wanted to have everything said before it was too late. 'The Chief-of-Staff appointed Major Farago to do the job.' The ghost of a grin crossed his ruined face. 'A bold one, that Farago,' he said, as if he were talking to himself. 'You see he speaks Czech and he has family here.' He coughed again. The cough seemed to tear his body apart. More blood appeared at his mouth.

Hastily Hardt wiped it away with his handkerchief.

'Thank you,' he whispered gratefully. 'You are very kind... In particular, Farago had a cousin here, the Countess Barek. She has a castle in lower *Erzgebirge*. Very remote. An ideal hiding place.' Now the dying Hungarian was finding it more and more difficult to speak. 'He left just after dawn ... this morning... Should be there by now. That Farago always was lucky. He missed the bombing...'

His body was tortured by the deep, agonising cough again.

'But what is so important about this Paper that you should go to such lengths to conceal it from the Russians?' Hardt asked swiftly.

'The Paper... Aach, it will show the world what...' he stopped abruptly. His bloody mouth mumbled something, which was lost in pink liquid but his single eye stared up at the two young American faces, willing them to do what he wanted. He tried to raise his hand. He never made it. Suddenly his head lolled to one side limply and he was dead...

Hardt stared angrily at the map spread out over the hood of the half-track, while behind him the men started to camouflage the second half-track with netting and branches, under Big Red's supervision. On the road a couple of the T-Force troopers kept air watch; *they* were not going to be surprised by the Red Air Force like the Hungarians had been. After the events of the last two days, Major Hardt was taking no chances.

'You know, Clarry,' he snapped, taking his eyes off the map. 'That *Erzgebirge* runs all the length of the Czech border with German Saxony, right down to the River Elbe and beyond. Hellfire, it would be like looking for a needle in a haystack to try to find a castle up there!'

'I don't know, sir,' van Fleet replied. 'Remember that poor Hungarian stiff said that this Major Farago guy set off at dawn and should have reached the castle by now. Okay, allowing him thirty miles an hour over the kind of roads which lead north, he should have covered about – say – a hundred miles in the four hours which have elapsed.'

'Yeah, I'll buy that, Clarry. A good point. And besides we can be sure that our mysterious Major wouldn't have gone east towards the Russians. So we can safely put his destination here' – his hand swept over the map – 'west of the Elbe.'

'Right, sir. And look at the road net leading out from here northwards. There are two major roads and a couple of minor ones which don't go too far. Now this one – here – runs to Dresden and we can be sure that he won't take that–'

'Because the Russians are already there,' Hardt said enthusiastically, as he realised that the task of finding the Major and whatever damned paper he had taken with him was not so hopeless as he had thought at first.

'So that leaves us with the major road to Karlsbad and then one of those minor roads which run north-east into the mountains.'

'Yeah, yeah, I'm with you, Clarry. But it is still one hell of an area to check out in the time we've got available to us. And, remember, I'm laying my Army career on the line for this. After all, we can no longer do anything for the Third Hungarian Army. The Russians have taken care of that part of the problem.'

'I agree, sir. But the Paper seems mighty important and you know it shouldn't be too difficult to find this Barek Castle.'

'How do you know! You've never been in this area in your goddam life.'

Van Fleet grinned impishly. 'Not exactly, sir. But do you know how my grandfather made his fortune in Boston?'

'Is that relevant at the moment, Clarry?'

'Please let me explain. It's so important. I think it'll make you understand better what I'm trying to get at, skipper.'

'Okay, get on with it. But make it snappy.'

'Well, you see it was like this. The old man made his pile by supplying five and ten cent stores with cheap glassware – crystal, *they* called it – vases, glasses and the like, the kind of stuff the old Boston Irish liked to put on show in their parlours.' He grinned again as if at an amusing memory. 'But in order to undercut the local competition, he imported, not to put too fine a point on it, cheap sweated labour.'

'Clarry I really don't see where this is leading us!' Hardt objected.

'Bear with me, sir. You will. Well, the Old Man imported that labour from the *Erzgebirge*. German peasant craftsmen who thought fifty cents an hour was a fortune and a twelve hour working day a rest camp. Now do you see, sir?'

'No, Clarry, I don't.'

'Well, those folk emigrated to the States because there was no dough in the mountains and no industry except the cottage industry of making glassware for peanuts. The *Erzgebirge* was and *is* one of the poorest districts in Central Europe. I conclude, skipper,' he said, confidently, 'there can't be too many castles in an area like that.'

Hardt absorbed the information for a moment. He nodded his head slowly. 'You just might be right there, Clarry.'

'I know I am, skipper. Besides Barek is a Czech name – the name of his cousin that is. And the locals on both sides of the frontier are primarily of German origin. So we can limit the field again there, can't we?'

'Yeah, yeah. You've sold me the idea,

Clarry. It looks as if we might have a chance of finding this – er – Major Farago after all.'

Van Fleet grinned happily, as Hardt began to fold up the big map. 'And if it's any consolation, skipper, if we run out of time before we find this Hungarian guy, we can always make a dash for Karlsbad to the west.'

'Why?' Hardt snapped, tossing the map into the cab.

'Because just before we left, I heard the Big Red One was about to take it, and anything the Big Red One decides to take, it does.'

Hardt nodded. He knew the reputation of America's premier infantry division, the First. 'Okay, let's not hang around here, shooting the breeze, Clarry. Roll 'em!'

Swiftly van Fleet ran back to his own vehicle. 'Get rid of that! Camouflage off,' he ordered, 'we're moving out.'

'Christ on a crutch!' Triggerman snarled angrily and threw the branch he was holding onto the ground. 'Can't nobody make up his goddam mind in this man's army!'

Hardt ignored the comment. He swung himself into the cab next to Wheels, who was already gunning the engine, while the rest tore away the camouflage with frantic fingers. 'Come on, you guys. Mount up! *Time's running out...*'

FIVE

But unknown to Major Hardt his time had already run out, for on that same hot afternoon, the Supreme Commander, fresh from the peace-signing ceremony at Rheims, made a sudden appearance at the Third Army HQ at Pilsen.

Hurriedly, and not a little apprehensive, Patton and Codman drove out to the airport to meet him. But Eisenhower was in a high good mood. 'Good to see you again, George,' he chortled and thrust out a big hand, his broad, moon-like face split by a grin that seemed to run from ear to ear. 'I thought I'd spend the afternoon with you. All I want to do is shake your hand, thank you for what you've done for the US Army, hand out a few decorations to your headquarters people and,' he licked his lips in mock anticipation, 'sample one of those liberated Czech steaks the scuttlebutt tells me you folks have gotten up here.'

'Of course, of course, General! Codman, don't just stand there. Rustle up the best steaks you can find in the whole of Czechoslovakia. At the double!'

Everything went well at first. Codman put up a splendid impromptu dinner, complete with tremendous Czech steaks obtained on the black market (although it went against the grain for a very proper Colonel Codman to obtain the food by such methods). Afterwards a happy, relaxed Eisenhower congratulated Patton on the achievements of his Army. 'You know, George,' he mused, 'you're not only a very good general, but a damn lucky stiff too. And you know what Napoleon said – he preferred luck to greatness in a commander.'

For one of the very few times in his long life, Patton blushed and mumbled something about the praise being 'too goddam much!'

But the trouble started when, just before his departure, Eisenhower thrust a list across the littered dinner table and announced easily, 'those are the names of your officers who I'd like to decorate before I leave.'

Happily Patton reached for his glasses to read the names. But what Eisenhower said next stopped him cold. 'You'll see I've put that young Hardt of yours at the top of the list. He really earned his DSC for his work in the Bulge!' Eisenhower lit yet another of the sixty cigarettes he chain-smoked each day. 'That boy needs watching – he's going places, George, believe you me.'

Patton licked suddenly dry lips. 'Ike,' he said hesitantly, 'I'm afraid he isn't here.'

There must have been something about Patton's manner which made Eisenhower suspicious. Abruptly his broad grin vanished. His face darkened. 'What do you mean, George?'

'He's just not here,' Patton stuttered like a schoolboy caught with his hand in his mother's cookie-jar.

'Then where is he?' Eisenhower snapped. 'He's part of your HQ, isn't he? What the hell is he doing away from it? This is peace-time, you know.' The grin, known to movie audiences all over the world had been replaced by a harsh frown; Patton knew the signs well. The Supreme Commander would explode at any moment and his temper was feared through the European Theatre of Operations. 'Goddamit, George, you haven't gone and gotten yourself in trouble again, have you?'

Patton bowed his shoulders. He could not let Hardt, an officer who had served him so well over these last years, take the responsibility for his own decision. Loyalty, he had always preached to his staff, does not only go upwards to one's superiors, but also downwards to one's subordinates. 'I guess, I might have, Ike,' he said lamely. 'You see it was like this.' Swiftly he explained what he had done, while Eisenhower listened, his eyes hard and angry.

When he was finished, Eisenhower, controlling his temper with difficulty, snapped, 'Jesus, George, don't you realise just what kind of awful doghouse you've gotten yourself into by what you've done? Not to mention the helluva fix you might have gotten me into with the Russians.'

'Always the purple-pissing Russians!' Patton exploded, angry with the Russians, angry with Ike, but most of all, angry with himself. His voice trembled. 'Day after day, Ike, some poor bloody Czech, or Hungarian, or Austrian or even German officer comes into my HQ. Hell, I've got to keep them from going down on their bended knees to me. And why do they come? I'll tell you, Ike. They come with tears in their eyes and they say, "In the name of God, General, come with your Army the rest of the way into our country. Give us a chance to set up our own governments. For pity's sake, give us this last chance to live before it's too late, before the Russians make slaves of us for ever."'

Before Eisenhower had an opportunity to protest, Patton rattled on, his thin cheeks flushed. 'That's what they tell me, Ike, and every damned one of them has offered to fight under my flag and bring their men with them. Hell, a German general offered me his entire air force to fight the Russians if necessary. Naturally he had hardly any planes left, but he had pilots. By God, I would have just loved to have taken him up on his offer! I felt a lousy traitor when I had to turn him down… Those people are right, Ike, and we're wrong. They won't have a chance with the Russians, and we have signed away their lives. By God, we ought to tear up those damned fool agreements we have made with the Russians and march right across their borders.' He gasped for breath and Ike seized the opportunity offered him.

'For God's sake, George,' he blurted out hotly. 'Now that's enough. *Enough*, do you hear! Haven't you had enough war by now?'

'I'll talk any damned way I want. I know what we ought to do. We promised those people freedom–'

'Be quiet, General,' Eisenhower ordered, his tone icy. 'Don't you realise that you're talking to your Supreme Commander?'

Suddenly the energy drained out of Patton, as if someone had opened a faucet and let it go in one great spurt. He sat back in his chair, his chest heaving, his breath coming in short, sharp gasps. Eisenhower looked at him. The war had taken its toll. Patton looked tired, very tired. There were deep, dark rings under his eyes and his face looked a lot thinner than the last time he had seen him.

'Look, George,' Eisenhower said, keeping his voice low, 'you know you are your own worse enemy. But I won't go into that now. All I'll say is this. From here on in, I'm not going to tolerate one more fool action like this from you. Make a horse's ass out of yourself again and you're *out!'* He snapped his thumb and forefinger together sharply. 'Now,' he rose and seized his cap, 'George, get those guys of yours back out of Russian territory at once.'

'But–'

'No buts! Get them back here at once and I don't care how you do it, even if you have to goddam well go out there and hand-carry them back yourself. *But get them back – NOW!'* And with that, he stalked out of the dining-room.

DAY FOUR

'You mean that Molotov got so drunk that he wrote out a paper detailing post-war Soviet intentions in Central Europe?'

Maj. Hardt to Maj. Farago,
May 9th, 1945.

ONE

'The Red Army!... The Red Army is coming!'

As the Guards Cavalry column started to move into the Prague suburb, sirens blaring, men, women and children streamed out of the houses cheering and screaming, extending their hands to husky Guardsmen perched on the tanks and half-tracks. Colonel Rurik looked down at the mob coldly. He had been told at his briefing that this was a working class suburb, but these men and women seemed too well dressed to be workers. A young man tried to keep pace with his command tank, crying in broken Russian *'Slava krasnaya armaya!*... Russians very good... I go with you...'

Rurik ignored him. He raised his twin signal flags and indicated that the convoy should speed up; they had no time to waste on the cheering mob. But another group of men and women in striped pyjamas had joined the throng and made it virtually impossible to get through. Rurik cursed under his breath. They were wasting precious time.

But the civilians in the striped pyjamas did not notice the angry look on the handsome officer's face. They came streaming forward, waving homemade flags, clutching pathetic bundles of garden flowers in their hands. Some were weeping and all were calling '*kommunista*' over and over again, as if it were part of some sacred litany. Slowly the lead tank ground to a halt.

'Who are you?' Rurik asked in Russian.

'We are communists – *communists,* Comrade General,' a skinny little man with a grey goatee and gold-rimmed glasses answered in good Russian.

Rurik looked down at him coldly. The man looked a typical middle-class intellectual who had gained his communism, not from hunger in his belly, but from the textbooks. He was a Yid to boot. 'And why are you blocking the street like this?' Rurik asked.

'To welcome you, Comrade General. We of the Party have waited six years for this moment. We have suffered.' He ran his hands down his striped pyjamas. 'This is the uniform of Mauthausen concentration camp.' He pointed to the red triangle on his breast. 'We are the politicals. Now you are here.' Carried away by sudden enthusiasm, he cried, 'Long live the Revolution! Long live

Comrade Stalin!'

'Long live Comrade Stalin!' the pathetic group of ex-concentration camp inmates quavered.

'Long live Comrade Stalin,' Rurik joined in routinely.

The man with the goatee began to weep suddenly.

'Typical Yiddish emotionalism,' Rurik told himself and asked, 'But why are you holding us up?'

'Because, Comrade General, we want you to go with us to Wenzel Square in the centre of the city. The bourgeoisie must see you and know that they have been liberated by the glorious Red Army.'

'Yes, yes,' a score of voices cried. Eagerly the mob stretched out their hands and placed them on the dusty metal sides of the Joseph Stalin, as if they were about to push it physically to the capital's main square.

It was at that moment that the command tank's lease-and-lend radio, the only one in the whole column capable of working over a distance, began to crackle urgently. Piotr, Rurik's radioman, pressed the earphones hard and began to read off the message as it came through, while Rurik ducked his head below the turret in order to hear above the cries of the mob. 'Air Reconnaissance … reports … American column sighted heading Route Five … towards Karlsbad… Recommend investigation after dealing with Hungarians…'

Rurik crouched there for a moment, absorbing the information. He knew that there would be promotion in it if he carried out this mission successfully, and Colonel Rurik was extremely ambitious. He couldn't afford to make mistakes. Could he, therefore, waste time checking the Hungarians when it might well be that the Americans were already hot on the scent of the all-important Paper? He reasoned that if they already had it, they would have turned and headed back to their own lines by the direct route. No, they were taking the Karlsbad road because they still did not possess it, but hoped to find it there, somewhere or other.

Colonel Rurik was suddenly seized by the old excitement: the thrill that was better than all the hunting and all the loving – the thrill of going into action again. In these last four years he had fought them all, Germans, Finns, Hungarians, Rumanians, Bulgars, Italians, even Spaniards. Now it might well be he would have to fight the Americans too, and he would defeat them like he had defeated all the rest. He thrust his head above the cupola and waggled his signal flags urgently. Behind the command tank, the other commanders rapped out swift orders. Rurik kicked his driver's back hard. *'Davai!'* he ordered, *'davai!'*

'But the civilians, Comrade Colonel?' the young driver protested earnestly.

'Damn the civilians!'

The driver gunned his engine. The civilians in striped pyjamas fell back in bewildered alarm. 'Comrade General,' the man with the goatee cried, 'You can't go ... please, you can't go *now!*'

'I can do what I like,' Rurik answered. 'And for your information, I am not a general, but a colonel, *Yid!*'

The man with the goatee staggered back as if he had been shot.

Slowly the long column started to move forward again through a suddenly silent mob of civilians, their tank tracks crushing the bundles of garden-flowers. The man with the goatee dropped the red flag he had been carrying. With his shoulders bent, he began to walk back to his house slowly. But Rurik did not see him; his bold eyes, gleaming now with excitement, were fixed on the road that led to the north-west and the confrontation that lay up there somewhere soon...

T-Force had been driving north all afternoon. The road had seemed an endless burning white, and their faces were caked with its dust, their eyes red-rimmed from its glare. About four they had seen the twin onion-topped towers of a Baroque church to the west and van Fleet had announced the place was Karlsbad. At the next crossroads they had turned north-east heading for the mountains, now a faint smudge on the burning horizon.

Slowly the endless fields of yellow sunflowers and parched maize began to give way to tight little patches of what looked like potatoes or turnips, planted in earth which was liberally sprinkled with stones. Here and there they passed tumbledown half-timbered farmhouses, which looked as if they had never seen a lick of paint or been repaired since they had been built a couple of centuries before. As Limey commented to Hardt. 'Cor, sir, yon folk look as if they don't even have a pot to piss in!'

'Yeah, you might just be right there, Limey.'

An hour beyond the Karlsbad turnoff, they came to a tiny shabby hamlet at a crossroads where the roads started to climb into the mountains in three different directions. Hardt ordered Wheels to halt and dropped stiffly out of the lead half-track. 'Well, Clarry,' he said to van Fleet, 'this is about as good a place as any to test out your theory about Castle Barak.'

Van Fleet wiped the thick dust from his face with an elegant silk handkerchief and nodded. 'Right skipper. But where are the locals?'

'Hiding, I suppose,' Hardt answered, turning to his driver. 'Wheels, hit the horn.'

The little ex-cabbie hit the horn hard, and kept his horny hand on the button until the peasants began to come slowly out of their tumbledown houses: bent old men, their faces burnt black and deeply wrinkled with hard work; old women in poke bonnets, dressed in black with blue overalls, their hands bent and swollen. Most of them seemed virtually toothless. Shyly, hands shading their eyes against the sun's slanting rays, they stared up at the tired young men on the half-tracks, whispering *'Amerikaner'* to each other. *'Es sind Amerikaner.'*

'Dutchie,' Hardt commented, 'ask them if they've ever heard of a Castle Barak.'

'Right, sir.'

'But don't ask them to scratch their heads,

Dutchie,' Limey quipped, 'or they're gonna get their pinkies full of wood splinters.'

The others laughed lazily and Major Hardt tried to keep a straight face. Limey was right – the peasants did look very thick.

Dutchie posed his question. But no one responded. The peasants stared at him blankly. A little helplessly, Dutchie looked up at Hardt. 'What now, sir?'

'Here, this is the way to do it,' Limey said abruptly. He dropped over the side of the half-track. Swiftly he pulled out a pack of *Camels* and offered a cigarette to the nearest old man. 'Here you are, old dad,' he cried very loudly as if he were speaking to a deaf person, 'clamp yer choppers – if yer've got any left – on one of these coffin nails.'

Hesitantly the old man accepted the cigarette with stiff gnarled fingers, examining it slowly, as if it might explode at any moment.

Limey did not appear to notice. Swiftly he passed out the cigarettes, chattering away busily in English all the time. He took out a couple of Hershey bars from his breast pocket and handed them to an old woman, whose face was almost hidden by a faded, well-washed bonnet. 'There you are, granny, tuck them under yer belt – they'll make yer eyes sparkle again. Perhaps you'll let granddad get in yer drawers tonight, eh?'

The old woman cackled like an ancient hen and abruptly the ice was broken; the peasants were prepared to talk. Still it was difficult. Most of them had not been more than twenty kilometres from the hamlet in their whole life. Time and time again Dutchie had to remind them of the name 'Barak'; and time after time it would set them off chattering among themselves in their incomprehensible dialect, producing names of hamlets that weren't even marked on the official US Army maps.

Hardt was just about to give up and order the column to move on when one of the old men, whose shabby black waistcoat was decorated by a heavy brass watch-chain, which probably indicated he was a little wealthier than the rest of the peasants, took one last loving draw at his *Camel* and announced in fairly High German: 'It's the foreigner!'

'Ask him what he means?' Hardt said urgently, clutching at straws. Soon it would be dark; they had no time to lose.

'The foreigner. I don't know her name,' the old man said doggedly, 'but she's a foreigner.'

'She!' van Fleet exclaimed. 'Did you hear that, skipper? The Hungarian said that Farago had a cousin who owned the property.'

'Yeah, yeah, I'm not that dumb, Clarry,' Hardt answered. 'Dutchie, ask him why he calls her a foreigner.'

'Because she is not one of us,' the old man answered. 'She doesn't speak German.'

'And where does she live?' Dutchie asked.

The old man shrugged. 'I do not know exactly. But in the old days when she hunted, she came down that road there' – he pointed to the road on the right.

'On horseback?' Hardt demanded. 'Ask him if she came on horseback, Dutchie.'

The old man nodded his agreement. Hardt turned to van Fleet. 'All right, you Bostonian nob, you. How far can you ride a hunter – in say a day?'

'We, the best people,' van Fleet grinned, 'wouldn't do much more than fifteen miles before giving the beast a rest.' He shrugged easily. 'But I wouldn't know how the commonfolk would treat their mounts.'

Hardt did a quick calculation. Say twenty-odd miles or so more and that would fit into the distance they had estimated the Hungarian Major might have covered by midday. A woman, too, who didn't belong to the local ethnic group and who hunted – obviously a sign of wealth. Put the two things together and it might just make the person they were looking for.

'All right,' he snapped, 'let's take a chance on it. We'll hit the track on the right. And Red.'

'Sir?'

'Break out a carton of C-ration and give it to the poor bastards,' he indicated the gaping peasants. 'They don't look as if they've had a square meal in a month of Sundays.'

'Will do, sir.'

Five minutes later the column was rattling up the steep incline into the mountains, leaving behind them the peasants staring down at the case of C-rations, as if it had just fallen from heaven.

And on the height, some five hundred metres away, the Fat One lowered his binoculars slowly, while the rest of them stared expectantly at his red, sweating face.

'What do you think?' Dieter Wagemut ventured.

'They must be onto something,' the Fat One answered ponderously.

'Do you think they're after the Molotov Paper?' the handsome blond Hitler Youth leader asked.

'I'm sure. They must have found out from the Hungarians. Why else would they be wasting time in these God-forsaken mountains, eh?'

The others nodded their agreement. 'I suppose you're right,' Dieter Wagemut conceded.

'Of course I'm right!' the Fat One snapped. 'I'm always right,' he said the words as if he believed in them implicitly. 'All right, let's not waste any more time talking here. We'll go down there and see what we can get out of those thick-headed peasants. After all, we have to look after our new allies, don't we?'

Laughing heartily the members of the *Kommando* ran back to the two trucks. A moment later they were rattling down the road, the noise the trucks made drowning the steady drone of the Russian spotter-plane hovering over the dark green mountains.

TWO

'Christ on a crutch!' Triggerman snarled as the half-track breasted the steep rise and they saw it, 'it's like something out of a crummy horror movie.'

Wheels braked and they all stared at the

castle, while around them the mountain fog billowed in the hollows of the forest, folding them in a milky grey.

The castle was a spiky black silhouette against the silver light of the moon and Hardt could not help but agree with Trigger-man as he surveyed the dark, silent structure. One could almost expect to see the Wolfman appear on its corrugated battlements and begin howling at the moon, or the long, dark sinister shape of Dracula come sailing down in search of fresh blood. Behind him Dutchie shuddered audibly and crossed himself hastily.

Limey laughed at him, but his laugh did not sound too convincing.

'What do you think, skipper?' van Fleet called across from the other half-track.

'Could be it, Clarry,' Hardt answered non-committally, 'but let's check it out – *the right way.*' He nodded to Red and Dutchie. 'You two come with me. You, Clarry, will stay here with the half-tracks and cover us. If anything gives, beat it! We've stuck out our necks too often on this mission, I'm not going to risk losing any more of the guys. Okay?'

'Kay, skipper. Message understood.'

Carefully, the three of them crept towards

the castle, their legs wreathed in the grey clinging mist. The castle was absolutely still. No light revealed the presence of human beings. Hardt reasoned the place would still be blacked out anyway. But as they got closer, the pungent smell of well-seasoned Central European food, which had Dutchie licking his lips in anticipation, betrayed the fact that the place was inhabited at all.

They circled the castle cautiously once, looking for an entrance. But the rear doors of massive, nailed oak were bolted firmly shut and all the ground floor windows were heavily shuttered. They circled the place again. Still without luck. In the end no other entrance was left to them but the great front door, surmounted by a worn stone coat-of-arms, the details of which they could not make out in the moonlight.

Gingerly Hardt crept forward across the gravel, while the other two, crouched low, covered him with their weapons. Taking his time, he turned the great iron door handle, which was shaped like a lion's head. Nothing happened. The door was locked.

'Balls,' Hardt cursed under his breath and wondered what he should do next.

'Trying knocking, sir,' Dutchie suggested in a stage whisper.

'Knock it off, dummy,' Big Red growled contemptuously. 'Who do ya think is waiting in there – the cruddy lady of the house, with a lousy cocktail in her pinkie?'

'I was only thinking–'

'Aw, you know what thought did – he shat himself!'

But in the end, Hardt realised that there was no other way of getting into the silent, forbidding place. Feeling an absolute fool, and still covered by Red and Dutchie, crouching in the bushes next to the gravel drive, he pulled the rusty chain of the bell. Deep, deep inside the castle, he caught the slow boom of a bell. For a while nothing happened. Hardt stamped his feet impatiently, his hand on his .45. Then abruptly there was the sound of heavy steps advancing towards the door at a measured pace.

'Stand by,' he rapped. 'There's somebody coming.'

The two GIs tensed, fingers on the triggers of their grease guns. Hastily Hardt loosened the flap of his holster and eased the colt into a better position.

The footsteps stopped. A pause. It was as if whoever was on the other side of the door was making some sort of ceremony out of opening it. A rusty chain was drawn back.

Another pause. A key rasped into a keyhole. Pause. And then finally the door started to swing open slowly on squeaky hinges which had not been oiled in many a year.

A grey-haired old man in an immaculate white jacket and well-pressed black trousers stood there in the sudden burst of yellow light that flooded out, his hands covered in white cotton gloves pressed tightly to his sides.

'Holy cow!' Big Red gasped. 'Wouldya believe it – *a goddam butler!*'

The old man looked at some distant object over Hardt's right shoulder, as if he did not notice the two heavily armed men in the bushes and said something in a language Hardt did not understand.

Hardt took it for Czech. *'Nix versteh,'* he said a little helplessly in broken German.

The butler slipped into that language at once. *'Sie wunschen, mein Herr?'* he queried.

'Countess Barak,' was all that Hardt could stutter.

The butler bowed stiffly at the waist and, with a sweep of white-gloved hand, said: *'Bitte treten Sie naher, meine Herren.'*

Awkwardly Hardt followed by the other two, entered the gloomy echoing hall. They had found Castle Barak!...

Just about that time, Patton finally received the message which ended a day of doubt and worry for him. Black Market brought it in personally. 'I thought you'd like to see it at once, sir,' he announced in his smart alert manner. 'It came in fifteen minutes ago from Bletchley via Ultra.'

'The Russians?' Patton asked quickly.

'Yessir.'

'Gimme it here!' Patton almost snatched the flimsy paper from his hand. Hurriedly he pulled out his steel-rimmed glasses and read through the message. It was the one that Colonel Rurik had received from his HQ that afternoon.

'It can only be T-Force,' Patton breathed out with a sigh of relief. 'There are no other troops east of the stop-line.'

'Yeah, just to be sure, I checked with the Big Red One at Karlsbad. They have no patrols out up there,' Black Market said smartly.

'Good thinking!' Patton said gratefully. 'And what about the Russian column that was at the receiving end of the message? What do you know of them?'

'Nothing, sir,' Black Market answered. 'Russian signals equipment is lousy, even at command level. For the most part they've been using our SCR-300 sets, which we let them have on Lease-Lend. But as you know, General, it is only line-of-sight in range, twenty-five miles,' he shrugged, 'perhaps thirty miles at the most.'

'So how do they communicate with each other say in an attack formation in tanks?' Patton asked, his professional interest in everything connected with armour, overcoming his worry.

'Well, from the Kraut signal experts I've questioned on the subject, they mostly use little flags.'

'So if you knock out the command tank and the guy with the flags, the rest go to pieces – every man for himself kind of?'

'Right, sir.'

'Okay,' Patton dropped the subject, 'so we don't know what the Russians are up to, eh?'

'No, sir. All we know is that they are out there somewhere over the River Moldau on the other side of Prague heading in search of Hungarians. According to the message, then they start gunning for our boys.'

Patton did a quick calculation in his head. 'So that might give us till dawn or perhaps a little later before they reach Hardt?'

'I guess so, sir. Though, of course, we

don't know where Major Hardt is heading,' Black Market added, his handsome young face puzzled.

Patton didn't enlighten him. He knew Hardt and he knew too that his deviation from the original route and mission had something to do with the mysterious Molotov Paper. But he wasn't telling Black Market that; the fewer people that were in the know, the better. 'All right, Black Market, many thanks. You've done a swell job of work and relay my congratulations to those Ultra Limeys of yours.' He gave the Major a thin smile. 'I guess there are still a few good Limeys around, eh?'

Black Market grinned back. 'Yeah. I guess so, General. Thank you, sir.' He turned to go and Patton called after him, 'give me five minutes and then send in Colonel Codman, please.'

'Sir.'

When the Major had left, Patton slumped back in his chair. It had been a trying day. From early morning, right through a burning hot afternoon, he had attempted to contact T-Force to get them to withdraw, as Eisenhower had ordered him to do. The HQ radio operators had tried every trick in the book to make Hardt break radio silence. To no avail. Twice he had risked sending out L-5 spotter planes over the no-man's land between his own Army and the advancing Russians. They had finally reported that the Third Hungarian Army had been bombed out of existence, but that there was no sign of T-Force.

At noon, Sergeant Holman had rolled in, the sides of his dusty half-track chipped with bullet marks like the symptoms of some loathsome skin disease. Patton had breathed out a sigh of relief when he had been informed and, leaving his lunch half-eaten, had rushed to welcome the men. But his gloom had returned instantly when a weary Holman, his head encircled by a bloody bandage, told the Army Commander how he had been separated from Major Hardt early on in the operation and how it had taken him all this time to fight his way back through marauding Cossacks and the like. Sadly Patton had dismissed the survivors, another hope shattered. But now he knew he was onto something after all. Hardt was somewhere far to the north in the region of the *Erzgebirge* mountains, perhaps thirty miles or so from the nearest US positions.

He rose to his feet and stumped over to the big map on the wall. Thoughtfully he studied it. With his right hand outstretched, he measured the distance between the Moldau and the Hungarians' position as last reported by the spotter planes. He measured it then against the scale and worked out how long it would take the Russians to get that far. For a moment he eyed the road-net running north from the Hungarians' positions, considering what road the Russians might take. He dismissed the Karlsbad one. He reasoned that the Russians might just be scared he would send some of the Big Red across the demarcation line to intercept them. He snorted contemptuously. The Russians didn't know just how much Eisenhower had tied his hands on that score. No further US troops would be crossing the line, or he would be out of a job. Eisenhower made that clear enough.

'So,' he concluded, talking to himself, 'the bastards are going to use the Dresden highway.' Again he made a rapid calculation, his lips moving in the manner of an old man, as he worked out his sum. 'Ten hours, eh.' He flashed a glance at his watch. It was now nearly twenty-one hundred hours. 'That means the Russians could make Hardt's position by about first light tomorrow morning.' He frowned. That wouldn't give him time enough to carry out the plan that was beginning to form at the back of his mind. Then he realised that the Russians would first have to find the T-Force men. At night their air reconnaissance would be blinded. Their Air Force did not possess any of the sophisticated devices used by the American Army Air Corps to locate small targets, which the two half-tracks were, even during darkness. The Soviet commander on the ground would have to wait till it was light enough for his recon plane to start looking for Hardt. That might take another hour. Patton's face lit up. 'By then, God willing,' he announced to the empty room, 'we'll be ready to pull them out.'

It was just at that moment that Codman knocked at the door in his subdued, very Bostonian manner. 'Come in,' Patton grunted, still pre-occupied with his new plan. The door didn't open. After a few seconds, Codman tapped again.

'For Chrissake, *come in!*' Patton rasped in his high-pitched squeaky voice. 'What in Sam Hill do you want, Charley? A goddam written invitation!'

Codman flew in, his face indicating he was obviously prepared for the worst – he knew just what a terrible, nerve-wracking day this had been for the Old Man. To his surprise,

Patton beamed at him across the map and said, as if he didn't have a care in the world. 'Charley, you're a former flyboy, aren't you?'

'Sure, sir. You know that.' Codman answered a little surprised. He and Patton had often talked about their experiences in France as young officers during the First World War; the Old Man knew he had been a fighter pilot until he had been shot down and taken prisoner.

'What rank did you make, Charley, before the Boche put you in the cage?' Patton asked and taking out one of his big Havanas, began to suck the end prior to lighting it.

Completely bewildered by the trend of the conversation, Codman answered. 'Well, at the time I was shot down over France, I was a first lieutenant. But they made me captain by the Armistice, sir.'

'Just a lowly captain, eh,' Patton said thoughtfully, his lean face suddenly wreathed in expensive blue smoke. He leaned back against the wall thoughtfully, one booted leg crossed over the other. For what seemed a long time he didn't speak. 'Charley,' he said then, 'how many L-5s do you think we might have in the area? I mean how many of them could we rustle up within the hour?'

Codman was absolutely lost now. But he

did his best. 'Well, sir, at a rough guess, I'd say that Fifth Corps up the road might have twenty-five or thirty of them on flying status.'

'Twenty-five to thirty, eh,' Patton mused, 'that would be about enough.'

'Enough – enough for what, sir?' Codman asked.

But Patton did not seem to hear. His face, still wreathed in smoke, was animated by new energy. 'Charley,' he said, 'so you only made it to captain in the Army Air Corps in the Big War. Well, Charley, you know what I'm gonna do for you now in recognition of your long and distinguished service in my command in the Second War?'

'No, sir,' Codman answered a little apprehensively.

'I'm gonna make you the Commander-in-Chief of the Czech Air Force. How about that?' Patton grinned at him expansively.

'But the Czech Air Force doesn't exist, sir,' Codman gasped. 'It hasn't for years!'

'Oh, yes, it does, Charley.' Patton's grin vanished and he was businesslike again. 'You see, I've just created it and you're gonna run it. Now listen, this is what we're gonna do...'

THREE

Major Farago was a short, dark, determined man who used his hands a great deal when he spoke, which was most of the time, although it was obviously a long time since he had last spoken English.

Now, standing in front of the great blazing log fire, which was welcome because the nights were cold in the mountains, he explained what the whole business was about. The T-Force men, balancing elegant china cups full of strong black coffee awkwardly in one hand and tiny glasses of fiery plum brandy in the other, listened to him. 'You are seeing, Mr Major that there were two of us who are friends of Miklos – we are calling him Mickey – Horthy last year when he deal with the Russians. Mickey, he was no fool. In the end he made Molotov – you know?' he enquired eagerly with a flash of those elegant, never still hands.

'The Russian Foreign Minister,' Hardt answered, realising at that moment just how beat he was.

'Yes, Russian Foreign Minister. So, he make Molotov come to meet him.' He shrugged. 'I know not where – somewhere in the Carpathians perhaps. Is not important. So, Molotov arrive. Big, heavy, slow.' Farago puffed out his cheeks to illustrate what he meant. 'Like these Czech *knoedli,* what you say?' He snapped his fingers in irritation.

'Dumplings,' Dutchie suggested.

'Yes, dumplings. All grey and starchy. But Mickey – ah, that Mickey,' his dark eyes twinkled at some private memory 'he know how to treat such a man. They talk all morning, all afternoon and then Mickey, he serves the Tokay and the champagne and *raki.* Molotov is same as all Russians. Cannot stop.' He threw back his head and thrust his thumb at suddenly open lips, as if he were drinking from a bottle. 'He keep on drinking and drinking. Perhaps he think we Hungarians can't drink like the Russians. He mistaken.' Suddenly he remember his own glass. *'Chin-chin!'* he called and raised it to his chest, level with the third button of his dark tunic, elbow extended stiffly at a forty-five degree angle.

'Chin-chin,' Hardt answered wearily. It was already his fourth glass of the plum brandy.

Farago downed his, as if it were water, in

one fast gulp.

Hardt did the same and was seized by a fit of coughing. Farago did not seem to notice. *'Nochmal, Josef,'* he snapped at the ancient butler, waiting stiffly in the corner. 'You too,' he raised his voice, 'you men drink too, plenty more.' He beamed at the tired, unshaven T-Force. 'Me, I am a democrat ... like your President Roosevelt. I have nothing against common ones as you are.'

'Oh, Christ,' Limey said, half-amused, half-annoyed. 'Listen to his nibs there.' He mimicked the Major's accent cruelly, *'I have nothing against common ones, as you are'* and grabbed the decanter of plum brandy as Josef creaked past. 'Here you are, granddad, give it me. Us common ones don't want yer waiting on us hand and foot like that!'

But Farago didn't notice. He continued immediately. 'So what now, eh?' He answered his own question without even pausing for breath. 'That cunning Mickey, he bring on the gypsies. They play. Slow, fast, sad.' He shrugged eloquently. 'The Russians – they are fools for such things, eh?' He looked expectantly at Hardt, as if the two of them together knew just how foolish the Russians were.

Hardt nodded hurriedly and wondered

where all this was leading to.

'And now Mickey has him where he need him.' He opened his hand, palm upward, fingers outstretched, to illustrate what he meant. 'Here, eh, you understand?'

Hardt nodded.

'The grey dumpling is soft and Mickey he can – er – do this,' he wriggled his fingers urgently, as if he were kneading dough.

'Mould him?' Hardt suggested.

'Is possible. So he do this and in the end Molotov he write the Paper – two copies – *in his own hand!'* Farago looked at him triumphantly like an amateur magician who has just managed to produce a white rabbit from his top hat, 'what say you to that, eh, Major?'

'But what–'

Hardt should have known the question was simply rhetorical, for without waiting for him to finish the vital, bright-eyed Hungarian was off again. 'It was tremendous, even for Mickey! He tell the Russian dumpling how after War One–'

'The First War.'

'Ycs, War One, with the end of the Double Monarchy, is a vacuum in Middle Europe which the Germans fill, eh, under Hitler. Now War Two is soon finishing. The Germans are finished, how will Soviet Union fill the vacuum. Hungary must know if she is going to want to sign separate peace with Soviet Union. And Molotov, he bites! He write the Paper.'

'But what was in the Paper?' Hardt broke through the never ending flow of words.

'*What?* Everything.' He tapped his breast pocket abruptly.

'Here, we have everything. Poland, Rumania, Yugoslavia – they are all going to be taken over by – puppets, you say?'

'Yes.'

'By puppets government when the Red Army is in control. Czechoslovakia too, if possible. Hungary?' He shrugged eloquently. 'Naturally Molotov, he lie to Mickey. No, he says, Hungary will have an all-party parliament, but the Communist Party is to be legal. It is not before the war, you see,' he added hastily. 'Molotov gave Mickey his word that Hungary would be all right. But it counts for nothing. The Reds are not gentlemen.'

'You mean,' Hardt asked incredulously, 'Molotov got so drunk that he wrote out a paper detailing post-war Soviet intentions in Central Europe?'

Farago beamed at him happily. 'Yes.' He held up two fingers. 'Twice. Gaza got one later and I–'

It was at that moment that the door opened. Farago spun round; then almost immediately he relaxed when he saw the tall elegant woman poised there. 'Elena,' he said, 'my cousin, the Countess Barak.'

Limey gave a soft whistle and Hardt shot him an angry look. But the woman ignored it. She advanced to Hardt and stretched out her hand in the continental fashion. For one awful moment, Hardt wondered whether he was expected to kiss it.

'Major, I'm very happy to meet you,' the Countess said in an almost perfect English accent (the Countess Barak had spent four years at Oxford before the war).

Hardt mumbled something and looked at her. She was tall and dark, with fine flashing black eyes. By American standards, her face was a little too broad and bold – it was the face of a woman who wouldn't crack up when the going got tough, he couldn't help thinking – but Hardt found it very attractive. Indeed he found himself staring at her, and he had to force his eyes away, saying to Farago, who was smiling at him knowingly, 'And what happened then, Major?'

'When Mickey realised the Germans, our allies at that time, were onto him, he gave the two Papers to Gaza and me. In March the NKVD captured Gaza. That is how they know that we had escaped from Hungary with the second Paper.' He made a gesture as if he were slapping somebody's face. 'Poor Gaza, they had little mercy. You know the rest. I escape to my cousin here. I know she help me, eh, Elena.'

'Of course,' she said quickly and squeezed his hand. 'And it's "would help me".'

'Did I not say that?' Farago inquired with raised eyebrows.

She laughed and her fine breasts trembled delightfully under the loose silk blouse she was wearing. Then she was serious. 'There was little I could do. I have already dismissed the servants except Josef – he just wouldn't go. I didn't want them here when the Russians come. Once they come it will be the end of all this,' she swept a hand around the room a little sadly. 'And I didn't want my people to suffer because of their association with me.'

'But the Russians won't stay for ever?' Hardt protested. 'It was agreed at Yalta to allow all countries occupied by the Allies self-determination after the war was over.'

She smiled softly at such naïvety.

'That is why the Paper is so important,' Farago broke in, unable to keep quiet for very long. 'Naturally the Russians will say it is – how do you say?' He said something in Magyar.

'Forgery,' she supplied the word for him.

'But the people who know Molotov, your State Department, the English, their Foreign Office, they will recognise his handwriting.' He smiled cynically. 'After all he has signed enough worthless contracts–'

'Treaties,' she corrected him.

'Thank you, Elena. Treaties in these last years and they will know what the Reds want – complete domination of Middle Europe.' He stopped and stared hard at the American Major, as if he expected some sort of reaction.

Hardt did not react. He was thinking too hard. Now he realised why the Hungarian General had come to Patton in the first place; it was not only on account of his Army, it was because of the Paper. It was political dynamite, and the Hungarian General must have known that Patton was the man best suited to set off that dynamite. In essence, the Hungarian wanted trouble between the Western Allies and the Russians because that was the only way to save his own country. That was what it was all about.

Hardt bit his lip.

'What is the matter, Major?' Farago asked quickly.

'I was thinking,' Hardt said hesitantly.

'What?'

'That if I managed to get you and the Paper out of here,' Hardt hesitated, as if he found it difficult to formulate in words what he was thinking.

'Yes?'

'That it could cause a lot of trouble. Besides how can one know that it's not a forgery anyway?'

'The handwriting – Molotov's own handwriting, *here.*' He tapped his breast pocket again. 'Your experts will know that. Besides, why bomb the Third Hungarian Army like that, eh? They could have easy taken us prisoner. No, they had to bomb us. Why? Because they are feared.'

'Afraid,' the Countess corrected him automatically.

Hardt did not respond. Suddenly he was aware of the full implications of what he was doing. Hadn't the world suffered enough in these last terrible years? Should he contribute to starting a possible new conflict?

'Well, Major?' Farago demanded, his keen dark eyes searching Hardt's face for a sign. 'What do you think?'

Hardt smothered a yawn. 'I think I'm beat. My men too. It's been a long day.'

'But we could get to your lines this night,' Farago protested. 'It's only fifty kilometres–'

'Ladslo,' Elena Barak said firmly. 'Can't you see just how tired the Major and his men are!' She touched Hardt's arm and their eyes met. Hardt flushed, suddenly oddly embarrassed like a high school junior on his first date. 'I'll show you and your men where you can sleep. Josef,' she commanded, and said something to him in Czech.

The old butler creaked to the door, and opened it.

'Okay, fellers, time to hit the sack. We're getting out of here early tomorrow morning.'

They finished their drinks and started to troop towards the open door, yawning openly. At the fire, Farago gave in reluctantly. 'Good night then, Major Hardt, till the morning. Me, I will stand guard.' He tapped the little pistol strapped to the back of his black belt, and nodded significantly. 'With the Reds, you never know.'

'Goodnight,' Hardt said firmly. He had heard enough about the Reds. He closed the door behind him with a bang, leaving a suddenly deflated Farago staring into the dying flames...

DAY FIVE

'One day the whole gang of those Americans will start running west with our assistance and they'll never stop until we've kicked them back into the Atlantic Ocean where they came from.'

Col. Rurik to Capt. Gregor,
May 10th, 1945.

ONE

It was nearly midnight when the watchers on the heights above the little hamlet at the foot of the mountains spotted the Russians. At first the shivering youngsters could only hear the rattle of many tracks and the growl of the engines as they laboured up the steep incline. Then the first massive shape of a tank edged its way round the bend, taking it squarely, narrowly missing the rock outcrop with its great overhanging 90mm cannon; and there it was black and infinitely menacing against the cold silver of the moonlight.

'Joseph Stalin!' the Fat One exclaimed, dropping the carrot he had been munching.

'Are you sure?' Dieter, crouching next to him in the icy firs, asked.

'Naturally I'm sure. The Stalin has basically the same chassis as a T-34, but it's bigger and has a larger cannon. No shadow of a doubt. It's Russian all right.'

'Do you think it's the point of the Red Army?' Wiebke asked, as more and more tanks roared their way round the steep, difficult bend.

'No, it is not. What would the Red Army be doing up here? They would stick to the main roads on the plain. No, no, they're out looking for our … friends.' He sneered as he said the word.

'I've just counted them,' Dieter announced. 'Twenty tanks and ten trucks of infantry.'

The Fat One did a quick calculation. 'That makes it about a battalion of tanks and two companies of infantry.'

Behind them a tousle-haired boy, who didn't look a day over fourteen whistled softly through the gap in his front teeth and said: 'Great crap on the Christmas tree, that's a lot of men! How are the *Amis* going to cope with them? There are only twenty odd of them.'

'They won't have to,' the Fat One snapped. 'We will! And in three devils' names, don't try to talk so tough, you little crapper, you.'

The boy's bottom lip pouted, but he said nothing. Down below the first tanks had come to a stop in the little cobbled square. Faintly they could hear the guttural commands in Russian. Yellow lights began to go on everywhere and someone called out fearfully in German.

'Come on,' the Fat One commanded, 'let's get out of here. Down there they'll soon be singing like the dicky birds. The Ivans won't waste much time on them.' He pushed himself up with a thick grunt. 'Let's get back to the others and see how they are getting on.'

The Fat One had picked the place well, even Dieter who hated him, had to admit that. It was an outside curve of the steep winding road that led to the castle, with the mountainside falling off to the right in an almost sheer drop. For a section of about fifty metres on the left the rock hung over the road at a height of two metres and to a depth of about sixty centimetres. As the Fat One had explained to the *Kommando* before he had set them working, 'If we plant the explosive right, with a bit of luck we can bring the whole overcrop down and completely block the road.' Then he had issued his instructions with that overbearing confidence of his, as if he were a trained mining engineer. 'Dig two boreholes parallel to each other every two metres, alternating the height. The first two at one metre, the next one at one metre twenty and so on. Now get those chisels out of the trucks and get to it.'

That had been two hours ago. Now the job

was virtually completed, thanks to the softness of the rock, and even the Fat One could not quite restrain a grunt of approval, as the sweating, dirty youngsters, some of them with bleeding fingers stepped back to allow him to inspect their work.

'Good, good,' he said finally and then began to rap out fresh orders. 'Get the explosive and some of that nitrostarch... Fetch the fuse-wire ... come on, air your arses, will you!'

Wearily the boys and girls ran back up the road to where the two trucks were parked. Under his direction they started packing the explosive into the holes, linking it together by the green wire, while the Fat One explained his intention in between bites at another carrot. 'We'll hook it all up ... on the same circuit... Once the Ivans poke their noses round that corner ... we explode simultaneously... That whole outcrop should come down ... and, with a bit of luck, we might get a real landslide going. Now come on, hurry it up will you, you bunch of sluggards!'

Finally they were finished and now it was the Fat One's turn to work. As always when it was essential, he could move with remarkable speed. Swiftly he touched the leads of the detonating wire to the little galvanometer, straining his eyes in the dim light to check whether the needle moved. It did, right across the dial, then back and up again. The Fat One muttered his approval. The *Kommando* had wired up the explosive correctly as they had been taught to do in their Werewolf training schools. The splices were in order.

The Fat One flashed a glance at the leads. All right. He twisted them around the poles of the blasting machine and screwed them down tight under the wing nuts. He tapped the wooden handle of the plunger. It was all right too. Satisfied, he rose to his feet and said, 'Well as far as I'm concerned, the Ivans can come any time they like now. We're ready now to transport them to their Soviet heaven, eh?' He chuckled. It wasn't a pleasant sound.

They heard the throaty rumble of a tank advancing cautiously up the slope in first gear half an hour later. The Fat One was on his feet at once, throwing the carrot he was munching over the mountainside to their right. 'Get under cover,' he ordered.

They needed no urging. None of them, not even the Fat One for all his apparent professionalism, knew the full blasting power of the explosive which they had packed into the holes all along the mountainside. Hastily they scurried to the deep drainage ditch twenty metres beyond the trucks. The Fat One followed, as if he had all the time in the world and poised himself above the detonating device. The sound of the tanks was getting closer now.

Behind him, crouching in the ditch, his face pressed against his hands which were placed on the cold earth so that they would take the first impact of the explosion, Dieter Wagemut said, 'Why in hell's name is he waiting so long? Why doesn't he do it now?'

Wiebke flashed a look at the Fat One, his gross body crouched almost comically over the box, as if he were suffering from a bad case of constipation. 'Who knows?' she said. 'Who ever knows what goes on in his fat head?' She bent her face to her hands once more.

The Fat One was not one bit afraid. His reason told him he should blow the rock down now, but his appetite for sensation conquered reason. He wanted to see an Ivan tank on the stretch of road below the rock; then he would blow it. It would give him great pleasure to see the Ivan pigs sailing through the air in their metal coffin. He licked his thick lips in pleasurable anticipation.

The first Stalin tank edged its way round the bend awkwardly, its long gun swung to their right so that it could clear the corner more easily. The Fat One placed his chubby, sweaty hands on the plunger, picturing the Ivans in the tank in his mind's eye. Little did they realise that they would be dead men in another few seconds!

The Stalin started to rumble up the road below the rock outcrop. The Fat One knew he dare not wait any longer. He pressed the plunger with one hard, smooth thrust. There was a moment's pause. Unsuspectingly the big tank came on. Abruptly the earth heaved. Above the Stalin the rock split. A boulder detached itself from the outcrop. Almost lazily, it began to roll down. Another followed. And another. Suddenly the whole rock-face was quivering and trembling like a live thing. The Fat One could feel it under his feet.

The tank driver saw his danger. He braked hard. The tank slewed to one side as the torrent of rocks swept down the mountainside. The Fat One heard the brutal rasp of gears. The panic-stricken tank driver was trying to reverse. The Fat One licked his lips in pleasurable anticipation as the whole mountainside came rumbling down. The Stalin lurched backwards, zig-zagging from side to side. Too late!

The sea of rocks swept over it. Like a toy the rock-torrent carried it over the side of the road. It flew down the slope, bouncing and bouncing and bouncing. Then finally the ear-splitting roar was over and, as if in a trance, the Fat One found himself walking slowly to the scene of the destruction.

His Werewolves had done a beautiful job. The explosive had clawed off about fifty metres of the mountainside, completely blocking the road. There was now nothing above but the raw face of the mountain and below, a pile of still smoking boulders. Down below he could still hear odd rocks bumping and bouncing as they rumbled to the valley. Now, he knew, it would take a very agile soldier to clutch his way across the rock face and scramble to the other side where the road began again. For tanks, the road was blocked for days.

Well satisfied, the Fat One took a carrot out of his pocket and munching it happily started to waddle back to where the others were beginning to clamber out of the drainage ditch.

It was just then that the tall blond boy in the earth-coloured blouse and baggy breeches rose from the undergrowth high above the road and raised the stubby, round-barrelled sub-machinegun. It clattered in his dirty hands. The first burst caught the Fat One in his gross stomach. He staggered, his eyes full of absolute disbelief that this was happening to him. *'Nein,'* he gasped in terror and thrust out his hand, as if to ward off the bullets, *'nein, bitte nicht...!'*

The blond boy fired again. The Fat One screamed as the burst kicked hard at the back of his head with the impact of a mule's rear hooves. The top of his head flew off. Suddenly he was zooming out over a dark, dark sea to disintegrate in a sheet of violet flame.

From all the sides the soldiers in the earth-coloured uniforms rose from the firs above the drainage ditch and began firing into the boys and girls below. A couple tried to fire back. But they didn't have a chance. The Guardsmen chopped them down before they could even level their weapons. Mercilessly, ruthlessly, they poured their deadly fire into the trapped Werewolves, sending them reeling from side to side, screaming in high-pitched hysterical agony, until there was nothing below but the dead and dying, twitching on the earth in their last throes. *Werewolf Kommando Funf* was finished.

Rurik muttered a gross Russian obscenity as he stared at the still smoking rubble which blocked his way and waited for Gregor, the Guards' Infantry commander, to clamber down the mountainside. 'Well?' he demanded.

'Horoscho! They are all dead now.' He grinned and shoved his hat to the back of his head in the Russian fashion.

'Damned Fritzes!'

Rurik frowned. The gesture always irritated him. Young officers like Gregor were always making it, having copied it from some second-rate heroic painting of the Civil War or one of the cheap wartime propaganda movies. He didn't like it; it was cheap and unprofessional.

'Still,' Gregor said, 'the ambush worked like a charm.'

'That didn't,' Rurik grumbled. 'Now how am I going to get my Stalins across that?'

'Good job you weren't up front with your command tank, Comrade Colonel,' Gregor said cheekily. 'We did at least save you that – er – *headache.*'

'Standard operating procedure,' Rurik snapped, putting Gregor in his place. 'Tanks on the road, covering infantry on the heights. We've been doing it since the Caucasus in forty-two.'

'Yes, Comrade Colonel,' Gregor answered, his grin gone. 'What is the drill now?'

Rurik looked at him. Gregor was a good infantryman. He had done so well at Kursk that he had been promoted in the field from sergeant to under-lieutenant by Rostmistrov himself. He could be relied upon, Rurik knew. 'Now listen, Gregor, this is what we're going to do. Just in case those Fritz peasants down there lied, I shall run a cordon along the roads to the west out of here, while you find the castle and deal with the Americans. If you don't manage to pull it off and they bolt for it, I shall be waiting for them.'

'But how do you know they'll move west, Comrade Colonel?' Gregor asked.

'It is obvious. West to their own lines.' Rurik smiled coldly. 'One day the whole gang of those Americans will start running west with our assistance – and they'll never stop until we've kicked them back into the Atlantic Ocean where they came from.'

'Yes, Comrade Colonel,' Gregor replied dutifully.

TWO

The faint rumble of a distant explosion wakened Major Farago as he dozed in the darkened hall in front of the faintly glowing embers of the dying fire. He shook his head, licked his dry lips and automatically looked at the green luminous dial of his wristwatch. It was nearly two. Then he remembered a noise had woken him. Rising quickly from his chair he crossed the room, opened the mullioned window and, leaning across the sill, pushed open the heavy wooden shutters.

The night was still. Nothing moved. The road leading up to the castle, its surface gleaming in the moonlight, was empty.

Farago frowned, puzzled. He was sure he had heard something. But out there, there was nothing to be seen. He shrugged and muttered something to himself in Magyar. Just as he was about to reach out and close the shutters again, he saw the soldier.

He was coming cautiously out of the trees to the right and there was no mistaking the fat sub-machinegun hanging from his chest.

He was a Russian all right!

Farago caught his breath and bent low. There were others in the trees too, passing stealthily from fir to fir like the grey timber wolves of his own homeland. The Russians were everywhere.

Crouched down he backed carefully from the window, hardly daring to breathe, and opened the door to the corridor, praying that the usually thrifty Josef had extinguished the light there before he had gone to bed. He had. Hurriedly Farago closed the door behind him and felt his way in the darkness to the bottom of the stairs. A minute later he had opened the door to Hardt's room and was shaking the Major awake.

Hardt woke almost at once and listened to what the Hungarian had to say, the words coming in fast, hectic, bursts. Clad in his shorts and singlet, he sprang out of the big wooden bed, his metal identity discs rattling at his neck, and crossed to the window. Cautiously he opened it and peered out into the darkness. 'Balls!' he cursed softly, 'you're right, Farago.'

'What now, Major?'

Hardt swung round to face him. 'I don't rightly know. The Russians are our allies, you know,' he added as an afterthought.

Farago laughed. 'They will kill you, you know,' he said in a matter-of-fact voice. 'We have the Paper. We know too much.'

Hardt knew the Hungarian Major was right. The sudden appearance of the Russian troops below had forced his hand. He had to get his men out of the castle and back to their own lines. But how? Hurriedly he started to get into his clothes.

'We go?' the Hungarian asked.

'We go!'

The Hungarian's face lit up suddenly. 'Good, good,' he said excitedly.

Hardt ignored the other man's excitement and obvious pleasure. 'Knock off the row,' he cautioned. 'Now, get the others woken … your cousin too. And, hey, don't forget the old man. We'll take him with us as well.'

'At your service, Mr Major,' Farago cried happily and sped away.

'Kay,' Hardt snapped, staring round their sleepy faces, which looked unnaturally pale in the light of the study's tubular lighting, 'the Russians have gone and gotten us–'

'By the short and curlies,' Limey completed the phrase for him.

Hardt shot him an angry look. But Elena, dressed now in slacks and a sweater, her hair tied up in a bun at the back of her head, had not heard; her attention was concentrated solely on Hardt.

'Well, they've got us in here and those boys out there look as if they'll shoot first and start asking questions afterwards. We'd better not kid ourselves. They're playing for keeps!'

'But they're our allies,' Dutchie protested plaintively.

'Yeah,' Triggerman snarled, 'then why are they setting up machine guns out there on the lawn? Tell me that!'

'Knock it off,' Hardt intervened hastily. 'Okay, we haven't got a hope in hell of getting out by the front. As Trigger says, they've got it too well covered. The back's better. They've got a couple of guys posted near the door and about a dozen other fellers fifty feet away in the woods. Now, as you know, we've got the half-tracks back there in the courtyard and we've got to have them if we're to get out of these mountains.'

'Sure,' Old Baldy's little driver commented, 'can't go nowhere without wheels.'

Wheels looked surprised when the others laughed softly at his remark.

Hardt hurried on. 'Now if we could get rid of those guys at the door, we might have a chance of making a run for it with the half-tracks.'

'But they'd hear us starting up the motors, sir,' Limey objected. 'It's real brass monkey weather out there for May. They'd probably not start right off–'

'I've already thought of that, Limey,' Hardt interrupted hastily. 'There's a slight incline running out of the courtyard and it gets steeper once it hits the track at the back there. If we gave the half-tracks enough of a shove to get them rolling, we could start them on the track, once we've passed the Russians in the woods. If we make it that far, we could let out the clutch and then off like hell down that track. Fortunately it runs west, the way we want to go.'

'That's a ruddy lot of if's, sir,' Limey said slowly.

'Yeah, I know, but it's the only way.'

'But how are we going to open the door, skipper, without the two Russians hearing? If it's like everything else in the place, it will be as rusty as hell and kick up a devil of a racket.' Van Fleet stopped abruptly, as if he felt he had already said too much.

'Of course,' Hardt answered. 'I've thought of that too. You see, we don't open the door from the inside, we do it from the outside.'

'Who's *we*, sir?' Limey asked apprehensively, already knowing what the answer would be, for hadn't he gained the admiration of the whole of T-Force on account of his ability to scramble up telegraph posts like a human monkey.

Hardt grinned. 'You – and me.'

Elena Barak's face paled suddenly. Her eyes flashed Hardt a warning, but he pretended not to notice. 'All right,' he snapped. 'Let's move it. The Russians won't wait all night, before they start something.'

From the castle's battlements the route they would have to take was clearly visible, as were the two Russians crouched in the shadows facing the door. First they would have to tackle some fifty feet of sheer masonry. But fortunately it was so old and weathered, that there were plenty of gaps between the grey stones which would make suitable handholds. Then there was some sort of a glass roof. A conservatory or winter garden, Hardt told himself, and wondered how stable the glass panes might be. Beyond it came the lower half of the wall. It would probably have plenty of handholds too. But they would not be able to use them; they couldn't risk the Russians perhaps hearing them as they sweated their way down. The last bit would have to be taken fast and in silence. That was why they were going to use the hooked rope for it.

Hardt licked suddenly dry lips, feeling his heart beating furiously like a trip-hammer. 'Okay, Limey,' he whispered.

'Are you kidding, sir?' Limey answered hoarsely. 'I'm ready to fill me breeches at any moment.'

'Come on,' was Hardt's answer. 'It's now or never.'

Together they lowered themselves over the battlements and their arms took the strain. Convulsively burrowing their fingers into the gaps between the stones, they went down inch by inch, jaws clenched, breath coming in short harsh gasps, nerves stretched taut with fear. Once Hardt's hand slipped and just in time he bit back a scream of agony, as the rough stone ripped off his nails. Sweating and panting, eyes dilated crazily, every muscle crying out at the unbearable pain, they gradually worked their way down to the glass roof. And then they had made it and were crouching there, chests heaving furiously, as if they had just run a marathon.

'Okay?' Hardt gasped finally.

'It only hurts when I larf, sir,' Limey

croaked, as irrepressible as ever.

'Bully for you, Limey.'

Hardt took a deep breath and tried to calm his racing pulse. He knew he hadn't a minute to waste. He must go on. 'Okay, Limey,' he ordered, wiping the sweat off his forehead with the back of his hand, 'stage two.'

Gingerly he placed one hand on the grimy glass surface. It squeaked, but didn't give. He exerted more pressure. The glass bent alarmingly, but still it didn't break. Cautiously he put his knee on it and let it have almost his full body weight. Another squeak. But the glass held. 'I'm off now, Limey,' he whispered. 'Follow at two yards distance – and over there. We mustn't put too much weight on one spot.'

'Roger, sir – and sir!'

'What?'

'How do I get a quick transfer to the Quartermaster's Branch?'

Hardt grinned. 'I'll make a note of it, Limey – when we get back to base.'

Hand-knee ... hand-knee. The stretch of bulging, squeaking glass seemed endless. They crawled over it as if it were made of fragile eggshells. Once a pane snapped. To Hardt it sounded like the explosion of a 75mm shell. He stopped, hand poised in the air comically. But nothing happened. No shout of alarm or rage came from below. The Russians hadn't heard. Forcing himself to be calm, he started to crawl again.

They completed the tricky manoeuvre without any further incidents and lay there full length in the gutter, which stank of bird droppings, their faces lathered in sweat in spite of the cold night air, sucking their lacerated, bleeding fingers and trying once again to control their breathing. The Russians were only twenty yards away now.

Hardt wriggled himself closer to the edge and stared down at the two Russians for a very long time. He studied them as they crouched there motionlessly, like a wild animal stalking his prey. Somehow he sensed that they were as alert and tense as he was. There would be no opportunity to catch them off guard while they dozed or relaxed over a cigarette. They were on edge too, waiting for the order to attack the house to come through.

Clumsily he rolled over and slipped the extra pair of socks over his combat boots. After a moment Limey did the same. In sign language he indicated that Limey should fix the hook to the parapet. Limey nodded his understanding and fixed the hook to the stone with infinite caution. Hardt nodded his approval and Limey took the strain for a moment. The hook seemed to hold all right.

Hardt leaned very close to the little Cockney so much so that his nostrils were assailed by the stink of his sweat. Cupping his hands around the other man's ear, he whispered, 'I go first. Then you.'

Limey nodded his understanding.

'Split up and come in behind them. We mustn't alert them, or the balloon'll go up.'

Again Limey nodded.

'I'll click my tongue. Like this.' He made the sound. 'Then we go in together. Use your hands or your knife. Clear?'

Limey nodded once again.

'Okay, then here we go.' He released his hold on the other man and wriggling forward, tossed the rope gently over the side of the wall. A moment later he had lowered himself over too, knowing that he had now made the last irrevocable decision. Now it was either death or success. Swiftly he began to clamber down the rope, the sweat starting up all over his body immediately. The rope whirred upwards through his open feet – he was going down that fast that he was not using his legs – and the wire binding tore at his palms. He could smell the stink of burning flesh. But he felt no pain. He was concentrating totally on getting to the ground without being seen. Above him the rope tautened. Limey was coming down, *fast*.

He hit the ground and let go immediately. He pressed his hands hard against his wildly beating heart. To him it seemed that the two men crouching only yards away must hear it. But they did not move.

Limey landed softly next to him, his breath coming in harsh, shallow gasps. He nodded urgently. Hardt held up his forefinger and thumb in an 'O'. They had made it this far without trouble; it was a sign of triumph. Then in eloquent dumb play, he pointed to Limey and after that to the left. Limey understood. Sliding his knife out of his combat boot, he crept off to the left. An instant later Hardt slunk to the right.

Now Hardt had dropped all fear. All the normal human reactions seemed to have disappeared from him. Now he was motivated by sheer animal instinct: the instinct for self-preservation – for survival. It quickened his reflexes, pumping adrenalin into his bloodstream, giving him fresh reserves of strength.

By this time he was behind one of the two Russians. He could smell the man's stale sweat and the stench of the coarse black tobacco he smoked. Slowly, gingerly, he started to move in on him. To his left, Limey did the same. The two Russians stared ahead intently, unaware that soon they must die.

Twenty-five feet ... twenty ... fifteen feet ... ten ... five... Surely the Russians would hear them soon! But still they kept their backs to their murderers. Hardt knew he daren't risk that last five feet. He straightened up, his heart beating furiously and took a good grip of the earth with his heels. He hesitated, then he clicked his tongue.

In that same instant, the two of them sprang forward. Like wild predatory beasts, they grabbed their victims. Hardt seized the Russian's conical-shaped helmet and pulled it backwards. The strap slid under his chin and down to the throat, strangling his cry at the moment of its birth. With both hands he tugged hard, thrusting his knee into the Russian's arched back.

Now he was no longer a man, but an animal. He tugged and tugged with a strength born of furious desperation. In vain the dying Russian thrashed and wriggled crazily to escape that murderous grip. But Hardt had no mercy. His head thrown back in order to exert extra pressure, his teeth clenched, his eyes seemingly threatening to burst out of their sockets, he was still choking the man when he was already dead, afraid that some last cry of a death rattle might betray them, if he released his killer's hold too early. Finally he was satisfied that there was no further danger from the Russian. Slowly he began to release the pressure, ready to exert it again at any instant. But the Russian remained slack and lifeless. Gently, almost lovingly Hardt lowered him to the ground. A couple of yards away, Limey had released his lock on the other Russian's throat and, pulling out the knife sunk into his back with a repulsive sucking sound, was letting his victim fall to the earth, too.

A moment later he staggered over to Hardt and gasped, 'the poor bugger didn't look a day over sixteen, sir.' He stumbled and almost fell, but Hardt caught him just in time.

Hardt couldn't reply. His heart was hammering away against his ribs and his chest felt as if it would explode at any moment. His khaki swollen shirt clung damply to his body and he was lathered in sweat. All he could do was grip Limey's arm, and with a finger that trembled violently, point to the door.

Like two drunks they staggered towards it wordlessly. With fingers that felt like thick clumsy sausages, Hardt caught hold of the iron door ring, while Limey took out the spray – one of Elena's old-fashioned perfume atomizers – and hopefully puffed several quick sprays of petroleum on the door's hinges.

Hardt took a deep breath and exerted pressure. Slowly the door began to open with hardly a creak. Suddenly Hardt was oblivious to his thudding heart and trembling limbs. His bleeding torn hands, ripped fingers and bruised knees were forgotten. All he was conscious of was that he had pulled it off. He uttered a quick prayer of thanks, and thrust the great door back to its fullest extent.

The others were waiting for him in the shadows behind the half-tracks, gasping hard from the effort of getting the two six-ton vehicles into position beside the door. Now the half-tracks had been lightened, all spare gear deposited over the sides, with the crews, including Farago, Elena, even the ancient Josef, ready to start pushing once Hardt gave the order.

Hardt licked his cracked lips. 'Turn on the ignition,' he ordered in a whisper.

Wheels and the driver of van Fleet's half-track did as they were commanded.

'Gunners behind the 50 calibres!'

Triggerman and van Fleet's machine gunner swung themselves behind the 50 calibres and moved them round effortlessly so that they would be facing the fir wood once the half-tracks reached the trail.

Hardt hesitated momentarily. 'Limey,' he commanded, 'get behind – er – Old Baldy.' Suddenly he realised that for the first time since he had raised T-Force in North Africa he had used the hated name, which was the crew's joking reference to his own lack of hair. Now it didn't seem to matter any more.

Limey did as he was ordered.

'Okay – roll 'em!'

They took the strain. Nothing happened. Big Red grunted angrily, the muscles rippling through the shirt around his massive shoulders, his face beetroot red with the effort. Slowly Old Baldy started to move. Its crew renewed their efforts. There was a rusty clatter of tracks as Wheels swung the wheel round. Hardt's heart threatened to stop beating. It sounded as if a whole armoured division was on the move. He swung round to stare at the firs, fifty or so yards away.

Nothing stirred. The Russians obviously hadn't heard the sound.

'More beef!' he whispered urgently, as the second half-track began to edge forward. He doubled forward and with his body extended at a forty-five degree angle like a ski springer, added his weight to that of van Fleet's crew. The half-track began to move more rapidly.

Hardt stopped pushing. He grabbed Elena by the arm and thrust her forward towards Old Baldy. 'Hop aboard.' He shoved her bodily into the cab. 'And keep your head down!'

He turned to Farago who was shoving mightily with the old man doing his best beside him. 'Farago, get in this one as soon as she's really going – and don't forget to take the old man with you.'

Farago's teeth gleamed whitely in the moonlight – he seemed to have several more teeth than most people. 'At your service, Mr Major,' he replied smartly.

'All aboard now,' Hardt ordered curtly, as the first half-track began to gather speed.

The crew needed no urging. Running crazily they pelted after the silent-running vehicle and scrambled aboard as best they could. Hardt followed and with his foot on the towing hook at the back, heaving himself onto the deck, where already the others were cocking their weapons and levelling them at the line of firs.

Behind them van Fleet's half-track started to gain speed too. Now his crew had stopped pushing and were scrambling aboard.

Hardt unslung his grease gun and waited. They were almost level with the Russians positions now.

'Stoi?' a thick guttural voice challenged.

'Friend,' Farago shouted in Russian from the other half-track. 'Don't shoot – friend!'

'Smart thinking,' Hardt told himself, knowing instinctively what Farago had shouted, although he did not understand the language.

For a moment the man who had abruptly burst out of the woods, tommy-gun at the ready, was fooled. Then he spotted the white star on Old Baldy's side. He brought up his gun. But he never completed the movement. Trigger pressed the butt of the 50 calibre into his shoulder and fired. Tracer stitched the air. The Russian desperately fanned the air with his hands and fell back into the bushes.

'NOW!' Hardt yelled in an agony of suspense, as more and more Russians began

running out of the trees, firing as they came. *'TRY IT NOW, WHEELS!'*

Wheels let out the clutch. The half-track shuddered violently. Its speed slackened. But nothing else happened. The motor hadn't fired!

'Oh, for Chrissake, come on, Wheels!' someone cried, as the first lead started to patter against the half-track's metal sides.

'I'm doing my best!' Wheels yelled and thrust the clutch home again. Once more the half-track started to gather speed.

A Russian burst out onto the road in front of them. He held a stick grenade in one hand, fumbling with the other to draw out the pin.

'Watch that bugger, sarge!' Limey cried in alarm.

Big Red who was crouching behind Wheels acted instinctively. He fired a burst from the shoulder, the lead cutting the air just above Wheels' helmet. The Russian crumpled onto the road, watching helplessly as the live grenade rolled towards him. For a moment it nestled against his heaving breast; the next, it exploded, lifting the Russian high into the air in a burst of angry red-yellow flame. When the Russian came down again, his body was minus its head, which was rolling slowly to the ditch like a football lost by a careless schoolboy.

The half-track bumped across the headless body and that same instant, Wheels let out the clutch again. The engine spluttered, but didn't fire. Desperately Wheels hit the gas pedal. The lead was coming in thick and fast now. The engine spluttered again. Then suddenly the engine was roaring crazily, drowning even the sound of the small arms fire and the angry cries of the Russians who knew instinctively that their prey was going to get away after all. Hardt flung an anxious look behind them. Van Fleet's half-track was gaining on them rapidly. It was obvious that his motor was working well.

'Move it, Wheels, for God's sake!' he bellowed above the racket.

Wheels put his foot down hard on the gas and 'moved it'.

Seconds later they had disappeared behind the next bend in the mountain track. They were on their way home…

THREE

It was dawn at Pilsen Field.

But, despite the fact that he had been up all night, supervising the assembly of the 'Czech Air Force', General Patton was as fresh and immaculate as ever. His face was clean shaven and his uniform was bright and pressed, as if he had just been turned out by his coloured sergeant, Meeks, ready for a parade. 'Well, Codman,' he snapped to his Chief-Aide, his breath fogging on the still cold air, 'how does it feel to be the C-in-C of your own air force, eh?'

Codman, clad in a leather flying jacket, shook his head in disbelief when he saw the twenty-five L-5s drawn up on the field, the white star of the US Army Air Corps painted out and replaced by the gleaming new multi-coloured roundel of the Czech Air Force. 'I just can't believe it, sir,' he stuttered and rubbed his eyes.

'You'd better, Codman. Hell I spent half the night in that goddam hanger over there, checking they did the painting right and all that stuff – and I can tell you it was draughtier and colder than a well-digger's ass!' He shuddered. 'My God, couldn't I just do with a hot toddy at this moment!'

'But sir, do you really think we can pull it off?' Codman asked hesitantly.

'Course we can,' Patton replied firmly. 'Those guys,' he indicated the pilots lounging next to the planes smoking a last cigarette before take-off and chatting softly among themselves, 'are some of the best pilots in the Army. They know the score. They won't let you down. So this is the deal. Once over the demarcation line, you break formation and fly low. If the Russians have got radar of any capacity – and I doubt if those Mongolian buggers know their ass from their elbow about such technical gadgets – you'll be flying below it. So, once across, you'll sweep to a depth of say twenty miles between here and Karlsbad. I've already talked with the Big Red One and they've set up ground control to co-ordinate the search for T-Force. When you find them–'

If, Codman felt, would be a better word, but he kept that opinion to himself.

'You will concentrate the whole of your Air Force on that particular spot and–'

'I know what to do then, sir?' Codman dared to interrupt the Army Commander. 'What worries me is what I should do if the Russians attempt to interfere.'

Patton grinned impishly. 'Why should they? After all, you're the Czech Air Force and the Czechs are Russia's allies. The only ally who is in dutch with the Russians at this particular moment is, I guess, George S Patton esquire.'

'But what if they do attempt to have a go at us?' Codman persisted, knowing that his 'Air Force' was totally unarmed save for the pistols that the pilots carried. 'What then, sir?'

Patton's grin vanished. He pointed his thumb downwards. 'End of your command, Charley,' he said slowly. 'End of you!'

While General Patton was making his preparations to find and rescue T-Force, Colonel Rurik had not been idle either. Just before dawn when he anticipated the appearance of his own spotting plane from the Ukrainian Army at the front, he had drawn up a stop-line across the handful of second-class roads leading out of *Erzgebirge* to the west. At selected spots on each road, he had set up a roadblock of infantry and tanks, linking them by truck-borne infantry patrols covering the intervening open country so that each stretch was checked at fifteen minute intervals.

But even these arrangements had not satisfied him completely; then he knew just how much was at stake. He had to intercept the Americans, if Gregor chanced to fail in his mission. Five kilometres to the rear, he had established a stop-gap roadblock with his own HQ tank platoon stringing the tanks across the fields on both sides of the main entrance road to Karlsbad, a matter of a couple of kilometres from the demarcation line. Now as he surveyed his tanks, well camouflaged in the metre-high maize fields, waiting anxiously for Gregor's radio message confirming that he had the Molotov Paper and had dealt with the Americans, he could hear the faint sound of reveille bugles coming from the American barracks in Karlsbad. For him at that moment, the urgent clarion call sounded like a call to action. Throwing away his long black Russian cigarette, he began to stride impatiently down the road towards a line of refugees who had popped up from nowhere as news of the Russians' sudden appearance spread like wildfire from village to village.

He would clear the peasant rabble off the road himself. His Stalins would need a clear field of fire if the Americans ever came over that rise.

FOUR

The sun flickered through the leaves now, casting long black shadows across the fields before them. Above, in the trees, birds twittered crazily and the first lizards of the new day were venturing out to bathe in the sun.

But the two men crouched under cover of the bushes had no ears for the birds, nor eyes for the lizards. Their gaze was fixed unflinchingly on the road some five hundred yards ahead. Behind them, driven deep into the protection of the trees, the rest of the half-track crews waited expectantly for their decision.

'Yeah, they're Russians all right,' van Fleet said, lowering his glasses.

Hardt spat into the dust. 'Yes, I thought they were.' He took his glasses off the little cluster of soldiers grouped around two tanks, one on each side of the road ahead. 'And you can bet your bottom dollar, Clarry, that the bastards are covering every exit road out of the mountains in the same way. They're putting on a max effort to get that damned Paper back.' Suddenly he wished he had never heard of the Molotov Paper.

'What are we going to do, skipper?' van Fleet asked after a moment's silence.

'Well, for one thing we can't sit here on our butts much longer. For all I know those guys back at the castle might have had a radio.' He shrugged. 'Hell they might have already alerted their friends up there that we're on our way. Welcome into my parlour, said the spider to the fly,' he said bitterly.

'We could abandon the half-tracks and try to slip through on foot cross-country,' van Fleet suggested hopefully, trying to shake Hardt out of his black mood.

'No deal, Clarry. We've got the wounded. Then there's the old man – *and* the Countess,' he added a little lamely.

Van Fleet lapsed into silence. There was no sound now save the twittering of the birds and the lazy hum of insects.

Glumly Hardt raised his binoculars and studied the Russian roadblock once again. He knew now that the Russians wouldn't hesitate to open fire on them – allies or no allies – and the half-track's inch-thick armour did not stand an earthly chance against the Stalin 90mm gun, even if they could get close enough to do any damage to the Russians with their personal weapons an unlikely possibility.

A truck cut into the bright circle of calibrated glass. It was filled with young men in dust-coloured uniforms, and there was a dull red star on its side. Also Russian, he concluded. He watched how the officer, with the heavy clapboards on his shoulders, exchanged a few words with the man in the cab before the truck turned and started to clatter back the way it had come across the dusty maize fields. A link patrol he told himself automatically. So van Fleet's idea of trying to break through the cordon on foot was out too.

Hardt bit his lip. They were only a matter of miles from Karlsbad now. They had to get through before the Russians got their spotter planes up looking for them. But how? In their American half-tracks they would stick out like a sore thumb on the little Czech roads – the only other traffic was ox-carts and ancient, wood-burning trucks.

Hardt swung his binoculars up the road

towards the wood in which they were now hiding. And then he spotted them – the refugees. Young men walking briskly with the aid of staffs; family groups, pushing their handful of pathetic possessions in front of them in buggies, wheelbarrows or towing them in little handcarts – in anything with wheels. Even at that distance Hardt could hear the squeal of long unoiled, protesting wheels.

Behind them came the farm wagons, ancient coaches, still covered with the dust of decades, wood-burning trucks, great, lumbering oxen drawing open-sided carts – it seemed as if all the barns in that part of Czechoslovakia had opened their doors and discharged their contents for this panic-stricken flight to the supposed safety of the American lines. Once these same people had called the Germans into the country. Now they were fleeing, knowing that soon the Russians and the Czechs, the despised Slavs, would make them pay for it – in blood.

Up ahead the Russians were stopping them here and there, looking for watches and other loot, while the men and women coagulated around them in a shrieking, crying knot. The Russians shrieked back in their turn. The officer with the big clapboards on his shoulders yelled an order. The soldiers lifted their weapons in both hands, holding them in front of them as if they were holding the bars in a gym, and began pushing the mob back. The pathetic procession started to move on again.

A minute later the Russians stopped the refugees again. This time they weren't looking for loot, though. They had surrounded a great rumbling ox-cart, laden high with hay and were poking their bayonets deep into the hay. And Hardt knew why. The Russians were looking for them!

Finally the Russian officer was satisfied. He indicated that the driver of the cart should continue. As the farmer whipped up his oxen hurriedly, obviously happy to have escaped with his hay (though Hardt wondered why in heaven's name anyone would want to run away with a cartload of hay), the watching Major lowered his glasses thoughtfully. 'Clarry,' he said slowly, 'I've got an idea. It's dicey. But hell, we're between the devil and the deep blue sea as it is! It's the only way out, I can see.'

Clarry van Fleet rolled over hastily and faced him, 'Go on, skipper,' he urged, 'spill it!'

'Well, it's like this...' Quickly Hardt

explained his sudden plan, while van Fleet listened, his face unusually serious for him. 'Well, what do you think?' Hardt ended.

'There are a lot of "if's" in it, skipper,' van Fleet answered. 'What if the Russians tumble to us too early? We'd be sitting ducks out there on the road.'

Hardt frowned. 'You are a little ray of sunshine, Clarry. But that's a chance we've got to take. Beggars can't be choosers – to coin a phrase.'

Van Fleet's face lit up. 'Of course, of course, you're right, skipper!' he snapped with feigned enthusiasm. 'We've got to get the digit out of the orifice. When do we start?'

Hardt looked one last time at the white gleaming road down below and whispered a quick prayer that he wasn't doing the wrong thing. 'Now!' he said.

'By the Holy Virgin of Kazan!' Rurik exploded. 'Did you have your hundred, man? How the devil did it happen, Gregor? *Over!*' He flicked the switch of the radio to receive.

Gregor's voice came over the air, distorted, metallic, but clearly unhappy. 'I don't know, Comrade Colonel. I had just got my soldiers into position, ready to take the place when they made a break for it in their vehicles to the rear. *Over!*'

'Which direction did they take?' Rurik snapped, telling himself he would ensure Gregor remained a captain even if he stayed in the Red Army for a hundred years.

'Westwards.' Swiftly Gregor read off the grid references.

'*Horoscho!* Now start moving westwards yourself, Gregor. Drive them before you as if you were driving game in front of you back home. We'll be waiting for them... And, by the way, burn that damned castle to the ground before you leave. *Over and out!*'

Angrily Rurik clicked off the radio and sat in the oppressive heat of the command tank's turret, absorbing Gregor's message. The Americans had won the first round. But by God, he would win the second, he told himself, his mind racing as he considered all the possibilities.

From what he knew of the Americans they would not abandon their vehicles and attempt to break through on foot. The Americans were soft; they didn't know how to walk like the Russians. No, they would stick to their half-tracks and that meant they would be virtually road-bound. The question now remained which road westwards to

Karlsbad would they take?

In the end he could not think of anything better than warning all road-block commanders that the Americans were coming. His handsome face set, he swung himself easily out of the turret and blew his whistle for the dispatch riders. In spite of the heat, the squat little men in their leather breeches and dusty knee boots came running. They knew Rurik's temper.

Swiftly Rurik, standing above them on the turret, rapped out his orders. 'It's no use trying to reach the road-block commanders by radio. So each one of you must take three road-blocks and warn the men there that the Americans are coming. If any one of them lets the Americans through this time, tell them, it is a court-martial for the commander and the penal battalion for the men. Understood?'

'Understood, Comrade Colonel!' they yelled as one.

'All right, off with you!'

As the dispatch riders ran to their machines, started them with a swift downward kick and were gone in a cloud of choking white dust, Rurik turned and stared moodily towards the east. Somehow, despite all the measures he had taken to prevent it, he knew the Americans would be coming soon, and that he must be ready to stop them. He dropped inside the turret and began to crank the great overhanging 90mm cannon round until its muzzle-break pointed directly at the road. 'Now,' he told himself under his breath, 'let them try to pass me!'

Slowly the great mass of hay, clearly visible above the plodding ox-cart led by a bare-foot peasant boy in front of it, came even closer to the road-block. The Russian peasant lads who made up the infantry of the Guards Regiment laughed when they saw it and made jokes about the stupid Fritzes who would be eating hay instead of potatoes in the coming winter and then continued their search of the group of young women, while the Joseph Stalins covered them with their guns.

The lumbering ox-cart was about fifty metres away, still covering most of the hay wagon, when the corn-blond sergeant with the Order of the Red Banner on his blouse heard the sound of the motors. 'What's that?' he called, raising his voice above the protests of the refugees, who were trying to protect their watches from the Russian soldiers.

No one answered. The soldiers were too busy with their demands for *'uris'*.

A little angrily, the Sergeant straightened up, taking his hands off the big breasts of a middle-aged farmer's wife, who was enjoying the 'search', while her ancient husband looked on glum-faced and glowering. 'Didn't any one of you dirty arses hear that?' he demanded.

A young soldier, busy strapping his third wristwatch around his brawny lower arm, made a crude suggestion.

'Your mother too,' the Sergeant answered without any particular vehemence, puzzled as he was by the source of the motor. His bright blue eyes flashed the length of the long sprawling column. Then he spotted it. The long green metal snout of the kind he had never seen on any farm tractor he had ever known. For a moment he couldn't believe his own eyes; then he cried urgently: 'Get your hands out of those Fritzes' knickers! To your weapons! The Americans are–'

The rest of his words were drowned by the sudden roar of motors and the chatter of machine gun fire.

The crew of Old Baldy had not understood the Russian sergeant's words, but they had comprehended their intent well enough. Together they heaved the mass of looted hay from the top of the half-track. As Wheels gunned the engine and broke out of the column, Trigger sprang to the machine gun and opened fire, while Limey flew to the radio and transmitted the agreed signal to van Fleet's half-track, some hundred yards behind them among the refugees.

Old Baldy rumbled across a ditch, narrowly missing a bare-foot boy herding ducks and sending his flock squawking in alarm in all directions. Directly to their front, the great gun was bearing down on them alarmingly. Trigger fired a swift burst. The Russians who had been searching the refugees scattered crazily. Wildly the half-track bumped across the field, crushing the maize. Lead pattered off its sides. But the crew didn't hear it. Holding on madly, their whole attention was fixed on the great tank. Now it seemed to blot out the horizon, as the gunner almost succeeded in bringing the 90mm to bear. Hardt knew he could wait no longer. 'Now!' he yelled above the chatter of the machine gun.

Big Red didn't hesitate. He pressed the trigger of the smoke discharge. There was a soft plop. The awkward-looking container flew fifty feet into the air. It was followed by another and another, whirling crazily, as they reached their maximum height and started to fall. In rapid succession they exploded just in front of the tank, as Hardt had hoped they would.

'Good shooting, Red!' he cried enthusiastically, as a thick grey cloud of smoke started to spread rapidly in front of the Stalin.

The gunner was blinded. Desperately he jerked his firing-bar. A huge spurt of vicious scarlet split the white cloud.

'Incoming mail!' someone cried.

They ducked as one. Hardt pressed Elena down to the dirty metal floor of the half-track. There was the sound – like a great piece of canvas being ripped forcibly apart. The half-track rocked violently like a ship at sea being struck by a sudden storm. Desperately Wheels fought the controls, cursing violently, the sweat streaming down his narrow face. The huge shell swept over their heads and they could feel its burning heat on the backs of their necks. Next moment they were past the Stalin and in the open again, rattling furiously towards the cover of the trees ahead. A second later van Fleet's half-track broke through the smoke and was following them, angry Russian bullets whining harmlessly off its rear. *They had done it!*

At the radio, Limey sat back hard in his metal seat and breathed, 'Cor ferk a duck, first the Jerries and now the Russkis!' He wiped the hay from his red face. 'What have I done to soddingly well deserve all this, eh?'

The others laughed, the tension broken. A moment later, they were round the bend and into the trees. Now it was only a matter of a few miles to Karlsbad and safety.

FIVE

Now the powerful spring sun was heating the earth and the heat columns tossed the little spotter plane around like a cork. The turbulence did not worry the cocky young pilot, with his little woollen GI cap stuck rakishly on the back of his head. Confidently he took the L-5 up a thousand feet, and as he did so, Colonel Codman, sitting at his side, could not help thinking that aviation had come a long way since a French pilot had given him his first flight in an open Voisin bomber thirty years before.

The air smoothed out. Under an empty blue sky, they settled down to covering the section of the map they had been allotted, flying slowly over rolling spring countryside, which seemed strangely empty of people and animals although there were white hamlets everywhere.

Codman was uneasy. In 1917 he had been shot by the Boche and wounded, but he had managed to escape with young Jimmy Hall. He had been young then. Now he was a forty-five-year-old retread; he couldn't be expected to do that kind of thing any longer. All the same he knew he had to help the Old Man to get himself out of the terrible mess he had gotten himself into before it was too late and he was fired from the command of the Third Army, as he had once been from the Seventh Army, back in Sicily.

Codman sighed wearily and began to search the ground below, moving his eyes slowly and carefully from left to right, using the technique he had learnt a quarter of a century before when he had been a snappy young pilot with the First Bombardment Group.

It was now ten o'clock.

It was just after ten that the little Russian biplane came sailing out of the sun in the east and caught the T-Force column completely by surprise. Wheels hit the brake automatically and Hardt was nearly flung against the windscreen.

'What the hell–' he began angrily, then his voice trailed away. He could *hear* the reason for Wheels' sudden stop. A plane was circling slowly above them.

Hardt grabbed his binoculars, while Elena stared at him fearfully. Furiously he focused them. The dull red stars stood out ominously in the glass circles.

'What do we do?' Big Red asked anxiously, cradling his grease gun in his enormous hands.

'Kill it!' Farago cried across from van Fleet's half-track. *'Kill it now!'*

Hardt hesitated for only a fraction of a second. 'Yeah,' he cried, 'knock the bastard out of the sky!'

The urgency conveyed by his order was contagious. Everywhere the weary T-Force men, even the wounded, raised their weapons and sent a furious hail of lead skywards. The little wooden biplane seemed oblivious to the assault. Despite the small arms fire, the pilot came in again to have another look. Hardt could see the red stars under its wings quite plainly. Furiously the machine guns chattered, the sweating gunners hanging onto the 50 calibres as if their very lives depended upon it. But their slugs went wide. Finally with one last contemptuous waggle of its wings, the biplane turned and started to speed towards the far horizon.

For one long angry moment, while the echo of the firing reverberated and died in the surrounding hills, Hardt stared at it. Around him his men resting on their blue-smoking weapons gazed at him anxiously, as the plane became a black speck and then finally vanished altogether.

In the end it was Limey who broke the silence. 'Did you notice, sir, which way it flew off?'

Hardt nodded glumly, realising the full implication of his observation. 'Yeah – *westwards!*'

They were only a matter of miles from Karlsbad now and the lines of the Big Red One. Slowly Hardt's uneasiness began to vanish. Perhaps the fact that the little plane had flown westwards after it had spotted them meant nothing. He relaxed. Another half hour at the most and they would be crossing the demarcation line and that would be that. Their last mission would be over.

He wiped the film of sweat from his face and, taking his eyes off Elena, who was sleeping with her pretty head resting against an empty jerry can, looked around at his crew. They had been with him from the beginning in North Africa, but in spite of everything that had happened since then, they had not changed much. Big Red was as red-faced and anxious as ever, looking as if he expected an attack at any moment. Trigger, leaning over the 50 calibre, had his face set in its usual dark sneer. Limey's expression as always, betrayed his normal mixture of cunning and good-humour. Dutchie, for his part, was the same old good guy who went to mass whenever he had the chance and disapproved of the sexual high jinx of the rest of the crew; as Limey had characterised him more than once 'a right old Roman Candle fisheater, who still believes in fairies at the bottom of the garden!' As for Wheels, his eyes concentrated on the road, he was treating the half-track as if it were a woman he loved, and there was an oil smudge on his narrow face. Suddenly Hardt realised he could not recollect ever seeing Wheels without an oily smudge on his face somewhere or other.

These were his men, who had followed him uncomplainingly on a dozen such dangerous missions as this, soldiers still, but soon – with the exception of Big Red, who was a regular – they would be civilians again.

Idly he wondered what would become of such men in civilian life. Would they ever be able to fit in again? How would they ever find anything to replace the kind of life they had been leading for the last three years? Could they react positively to the complications of civilian life when for years their existences had been limited to the next drink, the next meal, the next sleep, the next woman, the next sunrise – a life lived hour by hour and not year by year? And in the final analysis, how would they find in civilian life anything that would replace all this – the love and understanding of men for men in dangerous places and dangerous times?

Major Hardt sighed and suddenly felt very tired. He was glad that the mission was virtually over and it was peacetime at last. Yet, abruptly, he was afraid of that peace. What would it bring for them all?

The biplane came in low. Down beneath the

black figures grouped around the Stalin, with the red star identification panel draped over its engine, stared up at him in white-faced attention. The pilot waggled his wings to show that he had spotted them. Lowering his flaps and throttling back, he seemed to hover above them. With his free hand he pushed the cockpit hood open and dropped the metal container with the message.

At once the group broke as the soldiers streamed out into the maize field to pick it up. The pilot waggled his wings once more and then he was gone in a long bank. His job was over. Now it was up to the Army to deal with the Americans.

Down below, Rurik opened the cylinder swiftly and scanned the hastily pencilled message. Its contents made him angry, yet at the same time they pleased him. In the end, as he had predicted, it would be left to him alone to deal with the Americans. If the pilot's information was correct, they were now heading straight for him. He dropped the message and started to rap out orders. The Americans had come to the end of the road!

It was the disappearing exhaust of the Russian biplane – bright pink streaks against the orange disc of the sun – which accidentally drew Codman's attention to T-Force. Excitedly he nudged the pilot and pointed out the disappearing plane, which on account of the fact that it was a biplane could only be Russian, and in that same instant he spotted the two tiny vehicles crawling along the white road a couple of miles to the east.

Swiftly he focused his binoculars, knowing instinctively that it *had* to be them; there was no mistaking that characteristic long, drooping snout of the white half-track. In a flash the white star, clasped in a white circle, painted on the half-track's hood leapt into the glass. It was the mark of the Western Allied Armies. 'It's them, Lieutenant,' he cried excitedly. *'T-Force!'*

'Sure, Colonel,' the young pilot replied carelessly, wondering why the old boy was getting so excited.

'Well, get on the stick, Lieutenant!' Codman rapped, lowering his glasses. 'Contact Big Red One control and give them the reference – and make it snappy!'

'Roger, Colonel,' the young pilot answered easily. Almost lazily, he pressed his throat mike, while Codman fumed at his side with impatience.

Faintly on the still morning air, Hardt thought he could hear the sound of bugles beyond the hill. His tense face broke into a smile. 'Karlsbad, Countess,' he announced happily to Elena who had woken up now and was combing her beautiful jet-black hair as best she could with her fingers. 'That's the US Army, sounding officers' call. Now it's peacetime, we're back to the bugle.'

Elena smiled back at him, happy for him, but not quite understanding his words.

At that moment Hardt did not care. He was too concerned with getting them over the demarcation line and handing General Patton the damned Molotov Paper. All the same he felt as if a weight had been lifted from his shoulders. They were through.

Heartily he clapped his hand down on Wheels' shoulder as they breasted the hill. 'Okay, Wheels, hit the gas. We want to be in time for chow, don't–'

The words froze on his lips. In absolute horror as he saw the two tanks – barely visible, but there all the same – dug in, in a hull-down position on both sides of the road that led to Karlsbad. And there was no mistaking the red star on their turrets.

'Russian, sir?' Wheels gasped, automatic-

ally braking and pulling off the road.

Hardt did not answer. He couldn't! Slowly, very slowly, hoping against hope that he was mistaken, he raised his binoculars and focused them on the tanks some thousand yards away. But there was no mistaking those dull-red stars, nor the uniform of the tall officer, cap set back on his curly hair, long Russian cigarette drooping out of the corner of his mouth, his own glasses obviously fixed on the two half-tracks which had suddenly come to a stop on the top of the hill.

Thus for one long moment, the Russian Colonel and the American Major watched each other: the two veterans of the old war who were now new enemies. Then Hardt lowered his glasses and answered Wheels' question, his voice toneless. 'Yes, they're Russian all right.'

'What are you going to do, sir?' Big Red asked. 'Do you think they're going to pull something so close to the US lines?'

The Russian officer answered the second part of Big Red's question for him. Suddenly the man on the turret slid himself inside, pulling down the hatch-covers behind him expertly as he did so. They all knew the movement. The Russian was buttoning-down the tank for action. Behind

Hart, Limey said plaintively, 'Cor stone the ferking crows – *not a-bleeding-gain!*'

Hardt seemed mesmerized. They were completely exposed on the brow of the hill and already a platoon of infantry, armed with tommy-guns, was beginning to spread out in a long line through the maize, obviously waiting for the Americans to attempt to abandon their vehicles and make a run for it through the fields. His power of decision in the face of such a hopeless situation, just at the moment when he had felt they were safe, seemed to have abandoned Hardt. He struck his clenched fist against the palm of his left. 'Goddam,' he groaned, '*goddam!*'

'But, sir,' Big Red said desperately, 'what we gonna do now?' He wiped a big paw over his dry lips. 'If we don't–'

There was a tremendous roar. Below, the first Stalin shuddered violently. The great 90mm shell tore through the air. It exploded twenty yards to the right. Elena screamed shrilly as the half-track rocked and seemed about to overturn. An instant later they were deluged by a mass of earth and pebbles falling on their helmeted heads like heavy tropical rain. Now there was no way out. Almost calmly, Hardt prepared to meet his fate, as the second great gun swung in their direction. Using the stupid cliché of the time, he told himself fatalistically, *this was it*...

'Cut the engine!' Codman ordered harshly. 'For Chrissake, *cut the engine!*'

The young pilot reacted immediately. Like Codman he had taken in the scene at once: the two stalled half-tracks on the hill beyond; the fresh brown hole scarring the field; and the two heavy tanks, thin yellow smoke streaming from their muzzle flashes. The Americans up there were under attack!

Now they came gliding in behind the Russians, some two hundred feet below – silently, no sound save the rush of the wind against their wings. Suddenly the men in the earth-coloured blouses down amongst the yellow maize became aware of the little plane – and the myriad black dots behind it which were other planes. Some of them raised their tommy-guns as if to fire. But their commander had spotted the bright roundels under the L-5's wings. 'Don't shoot,' he yelled urgently. 'We have no quarrel with the Czechs – yet!'

Reluctantly the armoured infantrymen lowered their weapons. The young pilot seized the opportunity offered him. 'Thanks fellers,' he shouted, 'do the same for you guys one day.' Grinning broadly, he pushed the steering column down, his flaps down. The L-5's wheels hit the earth. A huge cloud of white dust shot up. The plane lurched violently. Its port wing almost touched the ground with the force of the impact. But the pilot caught it just in time. Shimmying crazily, trailing great clouds of dust behind it, the little plane shot through the maize and skidded to a stop, just as the second plane came in to land above the heads of the gawping Soviet infantry.

'Oh, my Christ, there must be dozens of the buggers!' Limey breathed, raising his head over the side of Old Baldy, staring wide-eyed at the little planes skidding to a halt everywhere in the bright-yellow maize field.

Suddenly Hardt woke out of his fatalistic reverie. He stood upright in the cab and stared at the planes. They were American all right, but their insignia was definitely not American. Were they some kind of Russian outfit?

That question was answered for him an instant later. A familiar hook-nosed face peered out of the nearest plane. Codman cupped his hands around his mouth. 'Hardt,' he bellowed over the ear-splitting racket of plane after plane landing all around, 'abandon those half-tracks and get your men over to the planes – *at the double, man!*'

Hardt overcame his shock, his heart racing faster in the knowledge that they had a chance after all; Patton hadn't let them down. 'Wilco!' he yelled back.

He grabbed Elena's hand firmly in his own. 'You're coming with me,' he cried, unslinging his grease gun with his free hand. 'Farago, you go with van Fleet. All right, you guys – *make a run for it!*'

The men needed no further urging. Frantically they dropped over the half-tracks' sides, taking only their personal weapons with them. Farago, one hand clasped to his breast pocket which contained the precious Paper, and the other holding the ancient St Stephen's Crown, dashed with van Fleet towards the plane. Hardt hesitated, shielding Elena with his own body, waiting till every man had abandoned the vehicles.

An angry burst of machine gun fire shattered the half-track's window. Glass flew everywhere. Hardt yelped with pain. He touched his cheek. His fingers came away wet with blood.

'You've been wounded!' Elena gasped.

'It's okay,' he answered and knew they couldn't wait much longer. The Russians would open up with their cannon again in a moment. His eyes fell on the name 'Old Baldy' painted in fading white paint on the half-track's side. Suddenly it felt wrong somehow to leave the old vehicle just like that – after all it had been a kind of home to them these last eleven months. Then he felt the girl's hand pressing his in fear and he knew there was no more time to waste.

'Come on – let's go,' he commanded and they were running, zig-zagging crazily, their shoes slipping on the maize, hearts pumping furiously, eyes wide and staring fixedly at the planes which meant escape – *life*.

The rattle of the Russian machine guns seemed far away. The slugs hissed through the chest-high maize all around them. But that didn't seem to matter. All that mattered was the planes. And then they had made it, blood pounding in their ears, their chests heaving frantically as if they might burst at any moment. Unceremoniously Codman pushed the girl inside. He followed himself. Hardt just bundled himself in, as the pilot started to taxi back along the side of the maize field. Everywhere the 'Czech Air

Force' planes were doing the same, followed by the enraged fire of the Russian infantry who now realised just how they had been fooled.

Rurik watched them go calmly, observing how the propellers flattened the maize in front of them and how the warm air rippled around the engines as they became airborne. The aircraft bounced across the rough fields, just skimming the green jagged line of the firs as they started their flight westwards. Lazily he waved to his men to cease firing and taking out a crumpled black cigarette forced the filter between his lips. With professional interest he watched the little planes join up in a diamond-shaped formation, become black dots on the horizon before they disappeared altogether.

So the Americans have won, he told himself. He accepted the realization without anger. He had lost battles before, but in the end he had won the war. He had lost this little skirmish too, but the war had only just begun and he knew he would meet the Americans again. Perhaps not this year, perhaps not even the next, but one year – he was absolutely sure of that. And then?

Suddenly he flung away his cigarette and

kicked his driver in the small of the back – the signal to start up. *'Davai!'* he snapped.

A minute later the 1st Guards Cavalry started to rumble back the way they had come – eastwards. But they would be back, Rurik knew that with the clarity of a vision. They would be back...

Two hours later Major Hardt, his face caked black with dried blood and accompanied by a grinning, if dirty and unshaven, Major Farago, was handing a beaming General Patton the Crown of Hungary.

With that typical romantic excess of his, Patton bent and pressed his lips to the ancient crown. 'One day,' he announced, 'I will return it in honour to where it belongs, I promise you.'

Farago's dirty face broke into a great smile. He knew that the Hungarian plotters had found the man they sought. 'General,' he broke in, 'I have something for you, which is being more, more important than Crown.' He pulled the sealed envelope which contained the Paper from his pocket and proudly presented it to Patton.

'What's this, Major?' Patton barked, a little irritated at being interrupted at this dramatic moment when the US Signal

Corps photographers, who were shooting the scene, had not yet taken a picture of him and the Crown of Hungary.

Farago explained in his swift if fractured English. For a moment after he finished his explanation Patton did not speak. Then he swung round to face Hardt, his faded blue eyes sparkling with sudden excitement, showing his dingy, sawn-off teeth in a broad grin. *'Holy damn, Hardt,'* he cried exuberantly, *'perhaps this ain't T-Force's last mission after all...'*

ENVOI

'The proper end for the professional soldier is a quick death inflicted by the *last* bullet of the *last* battle.'

Gen. George S. Patton, 1945.

But General Patton was wrong. It *was* T-Force's last mission. Two days later he presented the translation of the Molotov Paper, plus a sworn statement by a Republican friend of his who was a high official in the Department of State that the Paper was indeed in the Soviet Foreign Minister's handwriting, to his superior, General Bradley.

Bradley's reaction was totally contrary to what he had expected. His face pale, he stared at Patton from behind his GI glasses and cried, 'But George, you must be nuts to expect me to do anything with this! My God, George, don't you realise what a thing like this could lead to – a goddam third war!' He dropped the translation and affidavit on his deck, as if they were suddenly red-hot. 'Great balls of fire, I wouldn't touch a thing like that with a goddam bargepole!'

And that had been the end of Patton's attempt to make use of the Paper – at that level.

But the General did not give in so easily. Three days later he flew to Eisenhower's new headquarters in the IG Farben Building at Frankfurt to offer him the Paper.

Eisenhower read the translation through in silence and then placed it carefully in front of him on the big desk, which had once belonged to the head of the great German chemical concern.

'Well?' Patton demanded eagerly when Eisenhower did not speak.

'Well what?' Eisenhower asked through tightly compressed lips, his broad jaw working as if on steel springs, his face very pale.

'The Paper, Ike! What are you going to do about it?'

'Nothing.'

'But you can't mean that, Ike!' Patton protested. 'Surely, you can't. Hell, it outlines everything the Commies are going to do in Central Europe. They're gonna break every goddam agreement–'

'George,' Eisenhower broke firmly into Patton's excited flow of words, his eyes cold and stern. 'You frequently think everybody is against you. In reality, you have only one enemy in the world – *yourself!'* He eased his harsh tone a little. 'Now I don't want to sound like a Dutch uncle, but I've told you innumerable times to count ten before you take any abrupt action. You have persistently disregarded my advice, but it is not just advice any longer. From now on it's an order. Think before you leap, George, or you will no one to blame but yourself for the consequences of your rashness.' His voice hardened again. 'Now, I want the original of that Paper forwarded to Frankfurt by officer courier immediately you have returned to your own headquarters, and I want no more of this damned business. I'm trying to keep the peace with the Russians, not start a war. Once and for all, the Molotov Paper is a dead number. Do you understand, George, *a dead number!*'

Numbly Patton bent his greying head in defeat.

Dutifully Patton, who was still loyal enough to the Supreme Commander to know that he could not refuse his orders in spite of his reputation back in the States as America's foremost fighting general, forwarded the Molotov Paper and tried to forget the whole incident.

But he couldn't. Instead his anti-Communism and hatred of the new masters of Central Europe grew almost daily. Time and time again he refused to meet visiting delegations of Russian officers, and in private conversations with friends he attacked the

'Mongolian morons' as he was now calling the Russians. In the first week of September 1945, he was standing next to Marshal Zhukov, the burly Victor of Stalingrad, the Conqueror of Berlin, watching a military review of the four occupying powers. Huge Soviet tanks rattled by the stand and Zhukov, who Eisenhower fancied now was his friend, remarked through the interpreter: 'My dear General Patton, you see that tank. It carries a cannon which can throw a shell seven miles.'

Patton answered without a second's hesitation. 'Indeed? Well, my dear Marshal Zhukov, let me tell you this.' He thrust out his jaw pugnaciously, his eyes cold. 'If any of my gunners started firing at your people before they had closed to less than seven hundred yards, I'd have them goddamned court-martialled for cowardice!'

The Victor of Stalingrad's mouth dropped open stupidly. Patton's remark about his new friend did not go down well with Eisenhower, nor Patton's comment to his cronies that 'that eminent Tartar Zhukov has refused to accept Ike's invitation to visit the States unless Ike or his son John goes with him as a kind of hostage. It shows you the mentality of the Mongols. Totally dishonest themselves, they can't believe everybody else isn't.'

Eisenhower knew it was time to get rid of Patton. He was sick of Patton's reckless arrogance. On the morning of September 22nd, 1945, the opportunity he had been waiting for presented itself. At his first postwar conference he allowed himself to be quoted by eager correspondents out for a good juicy story as saying: '*American General Says Nazis Are Just Like Republicans And Democrats*' (thus the papers headlined the news the following day).

Patton refused to retract his statement in the form ordered by Eisenhower: the Third Army Commander was refusing to eat crow any longer.

Eight days later Eisenhower summoned Patton to his HQ in Frankfurt. There he was closeted with the Supreme Commander for two long hours, while the bulk of the press corps accredited to the Allied armies overseas waited outside for the result. When he emerged, Patton, dressed in simple uniform and minus his pearl-handled revolvers for once, was pale-faced and shaken. Eisenhower had taken his Third Army away from him!

On October 7th, 1945, representative detachments of the US Third Army paraded at the Commanding General's HQ at Bad Toelz, Bavaria to pay their last respects to General Patton. They came from every section of the once great Army – tankers and troopers, clerks and cooks were all represented. But the 600,000 strong army of veterans had vanished, returned to the States weeks before. Now most of the men on parade that cold but sunny morning in the former SS Officers' Training School were recruits, who had arrived in Europe after the fighting had finished.

Lt. Colonel Hardt, immaculate in his Class A uniform, four rows of ribbons adorning his left breast, two Purple Hearts and the Presidential Unit Citation on the other, threw a last glance at his own little detachment and realised that, apart from Big Red, there wasn't a face he recognised from the old wartime days. The others had gone weeks ago to be separated from the service. Some had gone of their own volition: Dutchie Schulze back to his 'Pa's farm' somewhere in Kansas; Wheels, eager to return to the New York rat-race and get back behind the wheel of a yellow cab – 'free ride for you, sir, any time. You'll find me at Grand

Central' had been his last words to Hardt; van Fleet, glad to be free of the fear which had haunted him throughout his Army career, returning to Boston's social whirl, 'the cocktail circuit' as he cynically called it.

Others had gone because they had been forced to go. Triggerman, afraid that the Mafia contract was still effective, had vanished the day he had been informed that he was to be shipped out. A couple of weeks later Hardt had received a picture postcard of Palermo with the message scrawled in a hurried hand on the back *'So long, suckers. T.'* Triggerman was running true to form!

Limey's departure had been similar. When he learnt from Big Red that the British military police had been making enquiries about a certain Corporal who had been missing from the British Eighth Army since 1942, he had requested an immediate seventy-two hour pass. 'To see me fiancée in Munich, sir,' he had explained to a smiling Hardt. 'You see, I think I've gone and got her in the pudden club.' He had smiled knowingly at his CO and Hardt had shaken his head in mock despair. Nothing would ever change the smart little Cockney. The last Hardt had heard of him through T-Force's grapevine was that Limey was running a whole stable of 'fiancées', working the busy circuit in the area about Munich's main PX. If any one of the T-Force made out in the tough, puzzling postwar world it would be Limey all right.

Now they were all gone. And soon Hardt would be gone too. T-Force was to be broken up at the end of the month and he and Big Red would be returning to the States for re-assignment. But at least he wouldn't go alone. He glanced across at the civilian guests in the roped-off area and smiled at Elena, his new wife, looking very pretty in her one and only black market outfit, obtained for her – naturally – by Limey before he had departed so hastily to see his 'fiancée'. Elena smiled back and blew him a kiss.

Hardt frowned, abruptly all West Point. He told himself that he would have to explain to her that army wives didn't do such things when their husbands were on parade.

Then he forgot Elena. General Patton and his successor in command of the Third Army, General Truscott, were mounting the reviewing platform. Patton was dressed in a tightly tailored combat jacket and pink gabardine riding breeches. On his head he wore his brightly lacquered helmet with its four outsize gilt stars. He was as immaculate and soldierly as ever, but Hardt could see that he clutched his swagger stick nervously, like a badly shaken infantryman after combat holding onto the cigarette which was the only thing that could settle his shot nerves.

Patton went into his last speech with his usual energy. 'General Truscott,' he snapped in his strangely high-pitched voice, 'officers and men. All good things must come to an end. The best thing that has ever come to me thus far is the honour and privilege of having commanded the Third Army.'

His faded-blue eyes swept the white mass of faces, as if he were seeing them for the very first time and he faltered for a moment. 'The great successes we have achieved together have been due primarily to the fighting heart of America,' he went on rapidly, as if eager to get the speech over with, 'but without the coordinating and supply activities of the General and Special Staffs even American valour would have been impotent... Goodbye – and God bless you!'

Fighting back the tears shimmering in his eyes, Patton handed an aide his swagger stick and took hold of his proudest possession: the Third Army Command flag, with its emblem of a big white letter 'A' set in a red and blue circle. Trying to smile at his old comrade, but failing lamentingly, he handed it to Truscott.

It was the signal the band had been waiting for. With a thump on the big drum, it stuck up in a spine-chilling shiver of brass, sending the black crows nesting in the dusty trees at the edge of the parade ground skywards in hoarse squawking protest.

'Third Army will ... pass in review ... pass in review!' The old, well-remembered, command echoed and re-echoed across the vast parade ground, fading slowly as the guidons moved out front.

The parade moved forward past the stand – unit after unit, which had given Patton the glory and the victory he had always sought. Time after time the order rang out: *'Eyes right!'*

On the platform, Patton swung each detachment an immaculate salute as if in his mind's eye he was seeing before him his veterans and not the callow, inexperienced youths who made up his units now.

Then it was T-Force's turn. *'Eyes right!'* Colonel Hardt barked.

Awkwardly the recruits clicked their heads to the right. Hardt did so too, his right hand shooting to his garrison cap in salute.

Patton stood there, eyes fixed on some

distant object, known only to himself, unseeing and unaware, the tears streaming down his lean old cheeks, as if they would never stop.

And then Hardt was ordering, *'Eyes front!'* and two paces behind him Big Red was saying in a hoarse, emotional whisper, 'Well, I guess, sir, that about winds up the old T-Force, eh?'

Hardt nodded slightly, not trusting himself to answer.

Thus they moved out into the cold autumn sun, the dust deadening the steady tread of many boots, their shadows lengthening across the parade ground behind them, as if reluctant to leave, marching out into history…

Rather more than two months later the General, who had always maintained that 'the proper end for the professional soldier is a quick death inflicted by the *last* bullet of the *last* battle' was dead. He had passed away quietly in his sleep – *in bed!*

The publishers hope that this book has given you enjoyable reading. Large Print Books are especially designed to be as easy to see and hold as possible. If you wish a complete list of our books please ask at your local library or write directly to:

Dales Large Print Books
Magna House, Long Preston,
Skipton, North Yorkshire.
BD23 4ND

This Large Print Book, for people who cannot read normal print, is published under the auspices of

THE ULVERSCROFT FOUNDATION

... we hope you have enjoyed this book. Please think for a moment about those who have worse eyesight than you ... and are unable to even read or enjoy Large Print without great difficulty.

You can help them by sending a donation, large or small, to:

The Ulverscroft Foundation,
1, The Green, Bradgate Road,
Anstey, Leicestershire, LE7 7FU,
England.

or request a copy of our brochure for more details.

The Foundation will use all donations to assist those people who are visually impaired and need special attention with medical research, diagnosis and treatment.

Thank you very much for your help.